In **Part 1**, Cyril F[...] plot that could destroy the world by plague. With the blessing of the British prime minister, Cyril and his trusted cohort, Geoffrey Cowlishaw, travel to Italy. . .to a top-secret meeting with Pope Adolfo I. On the way, Cyril and Geoffrey make some amazing discoveries and witness a dramatic self-sacrifice.

In **Part 2**, Cyril and Geoffrey discover the greatest obstacle to their top-secret mission: Baldasarre Gervasio, the pope's most trusted advisor, reviled as the "ratman." After Cyril discovers Gervasio's secret "experiments," he is followed into Gervasio's underground kingdom— the Roman catacombs—by a horde of trained rats who wait only for their master's command.

Now, Roger Elwood's
riveting six-part adventure
continues with. . .

PART 3
ACT OF SACRIFICE

Roger Elwood, whose gripping suspense titles have occupied best-seller lists over the past ten years, is well known to readers of Christian fiction. Such Elwood page-turners as *Angelwalk*, *Fallen Angel*, *Stedfast*, and *Darien* have together sold more than 400,000 copies.

A RIVETING SIX-PART ADVENTURE

PART 3
WITHOUT THE DAWN

ACT OF SACRIFICE

ROGER
ELWOOD

BARBOUR
PUBLISHING, INC.
Uhrichsville, Ohio

© MCMXCVII by Roger Elwood

ISBN 1-57748-038-4

Published by Barbour Publishing, Inc.
P.O. Box 719
Uhrichsville, Ohio 44683
http://www.barbourbooks.com

Member of the
Evangelical Christian
Publishers Association

Printed in the United States of America.

CHAPTER 1

Water slapping against rocks reached his ears, while the odor of fish assailed his nostrils. Other sounds. . .birds squawking overhead, someone gasping, footsteps hurrying. And a voice. A voice, it seemed, right next to him. . . .

"Lord Fothergill!"

It was loud, seemed familiar.

And then a hand. A hand touching his shoulder.

"Lord Fothergill! I must get you away from here!"

That same voice. More insistent this time.

Still Cyril could not respond in any manner, his aching body far too weak, with pain shooting through his back, chest, and legs.

"All of us are in danger if we are found here helping you! You must leave, Lord Fothergill!"

He struggled to move, at least to open his eyes, to find out who was disturbing his annihilation so rudely. Strong hands were grabbing hold of him. And he was fighting those who dared to invade his privacy, dared to try and change his destiny.

I do not want to come back, my blessed Jesus! His mind shouted words that his mouth could not yet utter. *Leave me here, oh, please, leave me. I expect the trumpet of the Lord will soon herald the opening of the gates of heaven for me. When this happens, I will be in His kingdom at last. Do not force me to stay in this mortal frame, this cursed world any longer. I yearn for the company of angels, especially the one who visited my father.*

Cyril had been rendered weaker than ever before in his life, and yet whoever it was who had their grip on him was proving very strong, a worthy opponent in some athletic competition, even if he had not had his strength battered from him.

He could feel himself on the edge of eternity.

Lord, how could You want me to return to such a world as the one I nearly left? A madman holds sway at the center of the largest organized church in Christendom! Rats may be poised to spread disease capable of wiping out tens of millions of people! Heathens may be waiting to pick up whatever pieces are left!

His eyelids suddenly shot open.

Liberatore! Alberto Liberatore was bending over him.

"Praise the Lord Jesus Himself!" the veteran member of the Vatican guard remarked. "I have prayed that the Lord would enable me to find you."

"Where am I?" Cyril asked.

"A mile from St. Peter's, on the banks of the Tiber."

"What happened?"

"You were swept out to the river."

"How did you find me?"

"I saw you being spewed out from the rear of the catacombs, and I followed you as closely as I could."

Cyril remembered that last image of Baldasarre Gervasio.

Looking like some bizarre oversized rodent, his hair short, his bare arms and legs, his skin almost albinolike, its pearly pastiness showing in the candlelight.

And the eyes. Tiny eyes. Tiny, bloodshot eyes.

"I am very cold," Cyril whispered.

"And I think you must be extremely sore," Liberatore reasoned. "It is a miracle that you seem not to have broken any bones."

Cyril could have added, truthfully, something else: "I have seen Baldasarre Gervasio and I want never to be in his presence again."

He could not admit to any relative stranger, even a Samaritan such as Liberatore, that his shivering was as much from fear gripping him as from the cold air of that Roman night.

The other man accepted what he said without dispute, adding, "It is near morning but still the air is chilly. You are soaked. I am not surprised that you feel as you do."

Cyril tried to explain what he had experienced in the catacombs under St. Peter's, but his mind was jumbled, his body so sore and weak that he could hardly move his jaw.

"Hell. . ." moaned Cyril. "A pathway to hell back there."

"It is a holy place!" Liberatore protested.

"No longer. Gervasio is remaking it in his own image."

"The bones of St. Peter are there. Surely God will strike him dead for any blasphemous acts."

Cyril fell silent. His hands had touched the remains of one of the greatest of the apostles.

Cyril stared at his hands, palms open.

"I have seen the bones," he said. "I have held them!"

"Tell me the rest later, Lord Fothergill. We must go. Surely Gervasio's stooges will come searching for you."

"You must not risk your life," Cyril said, nodding. "Tell me where to go and I shall leave now without the two of us being seen together."

"It is too late," Liberatore told him.

"Too late? For what?"

"You have been accused in the death of Eduardo Pintozzi, and a search for you will begin within a very short while."

"How could that be? He was killed by rats!"

Liberatore became unsteady.

"A very large amount of blood was discovered right in front of the main entrance to the basilica. And. . .and Eduardo's head was found just a few feet away."

Liberatore's face was drawn and he seemed to have developed more lines than just a day earlier.

"The rest of his body was missing," he commented slowly, "and may never be found."

"But if I were the murderer of Eduardo Pintozzi, why would I commit such a violent and messy act in so public a spot, and, fearing discovery, as I surely would, be so sloppy by leaving any part of his body behind, let alone Pintozzi's head?"

Liberatore paused, both cheeks twitching.

"Witnesses," he muttered with great reluctance. "You were supposed to have been surprised by witnesses."

"False witnesses, of course," Cyril replied. "I must testify directly to Adolfo. I must make sure that he understands the truth. I cannot believe a man of his undisputed intelligence would seriously regard anyone's word but mine."

Liberatore was shaking his head and frowning deeply.

"No one in the Vatican would believe you, Lord Fothergill," he went on to say. "That is startling but very true."

Cyril protested the notion that a man of his reputation would ever be considered a common liar.

"I have high credibility," he said, his voice raising in volume. "And I am here under the express protection of Prime Minister Edling."

"It is complicated, Lord Fothergill, more complicated than that," Liberatore told him, more uncomfortable than ever.

"You must be wrong. Edling—"

"It also has to do with Lord Cowlishaw."

"Geoffrey? He—"

"Dead, Lord Fothergill. . .he was murdered."

Cyril fell back with a groan, and Liberatore caught and held him tightly.

"I feel very faint," he said, panicking. "I think that I shall . . .die. . .if God has any mercy left!"

"No, Lord Fothergill, you will not die. Whatever brought you here must be so important that even Lord Cowlishaw's death should not stop you."

"He was so fine," Cyril mumbled nearly incoherently. "I came to think of Geoffrey as a dear brother."

"It is, I have to tell you, Lord Fothergill, far worse than it seems," Liberatore stated rather formally.

"Worse than what happened to this extraordinary man?"

"You are being blamed for his murder as well," Liberatore said, looking him full in the face.

Cyril did not blink, every muscle frozen, hearing these words that seemed beyond the most strained reasoning or presumption.

"But that is nothing less than lunacy," he said. "I had no motive whatever. We had only recently met but we became good friends. Geoffrey and I were here together because of—"

Cyril stopped, still aware of the need for the secrecy that Edling had imposed, and with which he continued to agree.

Liberatore's response was reluctant and pained.

"It seems that Gervasio has been successful in covincing the holy father that you and Lord Cowlishaw were lovers."

Of all the possible charges that could have been leveled against Cyril and Geoffrey, this one was the most preposterous and also the most devastating, despite an era of increasing tolerance of once forbidden lifestyles.

"And that I murdered him?"

"After a quarrel following Pintozzi's death. You found some rats and threw Lord Cowlishaw's body into their midst after you had rendered him unconscious. Soon the smell of blood and flesh attracted many times the original number of rats. There was little left of Lord Cowlishaw's body by the time—"

Cyril could only remember what he had seen of Eduardo Pintozzi's body, covered by gorging creatures, seconds before he turned down that alley.

"Geoffrey. . .Geoffrey. . .my new friend. . .oh, but my dear, dear friend!" Cyril cried out in anguish.

Dizzy and startled, he then became sick to his stomach, and lost any food that remained in it. After the heaving had finally passed, Liberatore sat down and held him, Cyril submitting unashamedly to this, grateful instead that he did have someone.

"You and I. . . .we can hide out in the countryside," the younger man said consolingly. "I have friends, you know, the most loyal friends, even in the midst of this chaos. They will gladly protect us until we decide what to do."

Cyril was recovering a measure of stability, but not quite ready to speak until minutes later.

"But we must do a great deal more than that," he said

finally. "We must get away altogether from Gervasio's influence."

He thought of the only escape route open to them.

"Cherbourg, yes, yes, we must head there right now. I can hire a seagoing vessel on the strength of my name alone."

His eyes opened wide as he considered that.

"Word could not spread that far faster than we are able to get to the seaport ourselves. After crossing the channel, we will have sanctuary in England."

Liberatore found this appealing.

"I have no family to be responsible for," he mused. "And I have never been beyond the borders of Italy. Besides, we may have no other choice. But what about that mission of yours, Lord Fothergill? Surely you were not able to complete it?"

"I was not," Cyril said, shaking his head.

The aftermath of his failure was clear.

"England must go ahead on her own, unless Edling enlists the aid of other leaders."

"I have a first cousin who is close to influential members of the French government," Liberatore offered. "He would cooperate if I asked him, and, I am quite sure, be very useful in helping us reach the right people around his own president."

"Good, good. Any such relationships will be needed. Adolfo could have been so helpful. But now we must make sure that he is not as indispensable as we thought before this trip began. Eventually he will have to go along."

"Not if Gervasio can help it, Lord Fothergill."

"But reality will have to set in."

Seeing Liberatore's blank look, Cyril decided to mention what had brought him from the safety of his native England all the way to Italy.

"I think you have earned the right to know some details," he relented, "if not all of them."

"I am honored that you have come to trust me enough to want to tell me," Liberatore replied earnestly, "but perhaps we should talk on the way to Cherbourg."

Cyril nodded willingly.

"I have an old Fiat nearby," Liberatore said. "I also have procured some hooded robes as disguises."

He chuckled a bit as the sight of the two of them in that garb crossed his mind.

"We will look like monks!" he joked. "Will that not be something, Lord Fothergill?"

Minutes later, on their way, Cyril began telling Alberto Liberatore about the Hanta virus.

Cyril Fothergill was finishing his recounting of events just as the middle of the morning approached.

"Men are capable of this?" Liberatore asked, dumbfounded, the information overwhelming. "A monsignor within the Holy See has become part of it?"

"I am more convinced than ever," Cyril assured him. "The evil that men do is greater than what either of us could realize since our minds, while not sinless, do not wallow in debauchery. We are not consumed by revenge. We do not desire the pain of millions."

What Cyril was telling him hit Alberto Liberatore especially hard.

"Desiring the pain of millions. . ." he repeated. "Is that what Gervasio and the others want?"

"It is not just a means to an end with their kind. Nor is it a necessary evil either, as the expression goes. I have reason to believe that the pain of millions is a large part of what they covet. They crave this pain for the infidels whom they consider their enemies! As far as the Muslim radicals involved are concerned, they can scarcely wait to stand in the middle of Paris or Rome or London and, to their delight, find these cities empty of infidel life."

A look of alarm and abhorrence captured Cyril's face.

"I can see their kind dancing on the tops of tables, celebrating the disposal of the bodies of men, women, and helpless children."

"But exposing themselves like that, would they not also

catch the virus?" Liberatore asked reasonably. "I have heard that suicide can be a weapon of theirs. But what do they gain if they wipe out themselves at the same time as their adversaries?"

Cyril considered that a reasonable question and pondered it for some while.

"I think they will not sweep over the conquered lands immediately. They will wait."

"But the stench, the appalling gruesomeness would be unbearable," Liberatore pointed out, his lips curled up in disgust. "How could even they stand it?"

Cyril's expression mirrored his own.

"You can be sure they would not be there at the beginning, too messy for them, too repugnant."

"The common soldier," Liberatore interjected, "those who are expendable, made stupid by their delusion."

"Absolutely!" Cyril agreed. "The radicals would send in the foot soldiers, the poor voiceless minions who have pledged devotion to Allah even if his supposed spokesmen ask what would be the impossible under other circumstances.

"That is, I daresay, an advantage they have over us. Their followers—whether civilians or of the military—have become mindless souls, having no authority of their own, no channels of resistance, no way to protest."

"So they send brave men to their deaths?" Liberatore asked. "Are they so barbaric as that?"

"Frankly it would not be as thoughtlessly dangerous as it might seem to us now. For I have to believe that the cleaning up stage would be reached only later, when the germs causing the hantavirus are long dead, and it is safe again to venture into the cities. Patience has always been one of their virtues, one that western Europeans have not had to the same degree.

"Every epidemic of disease throughout history has ultimately run its course. Germs are not eternal. In fact, they seem to have a short life span if they have nowhere to go and are left without a host to nourish them. If this did not happen to be the case, then there would be no life left in this world anywhere. We all would find ourselves at the mercy of an enemy unbeatable."

"I have known some Muslims," Liberatore commented, "and chatted with them as I performed my duties. They seem reasonable. They seem honest and soft-spoken."

"Most are, I suspect," Cyril agreed. "Most would find the actions of a radical few completely abhorrent, a betrayal of Islam. Whatever we might say about their beliefs, whatever we might think about their spiritual condition, we have to acknowledge that the great majority would never embrace the more violent passages of the Koran. Remember this: The plans of certain radicals precipitated the Crusades in the first place."

"What do we do now?"

Desperation had squeezed Liberatore's now fragile voice until it was hoarse.

Cyril was not sure what to say because getting through Italy and across France to Cherbourg was a journey that seemed destined to doom the two of them.

Surely Gervasio will fight us every step of the way, he told himself. *Surely he will have stooges waiting to spot us and—*

Then an alternative plan poked its way into his mind.

He assumes that I am dead, Cyril thought. *How could any man be expected to survive such an ordeal? Why waste favors and manpower, even if my body cannot be found?*

He found himself allowing a little smile.

Gervasio might visualize me being carried out to sea where a swarm of Mediterranean sharks would make short order of me. In any event, I would no longer be a threat to his clandestine reign with such charges as there were against me!

"We will be safe in England," Cyril finally said, "though how much longer my beloved England itself is going to be safe is another matter."

Surrounded by vast expanses of water for thousands of years, the British Isles did seem impregnable so long as

Edling's armed forces were capable of keeping out any unwanted visitors, human, animal, and rodent alike.

"To be safe before a faceless enemy?" Liberatore remarked ironically. "Is that possible, sir?"

He looked ahead, his eyes figuratively searching the future as much as the countryside itself.

"Do the heathen hordes not have the perfect weapon to use against us?" Liberatore posed. "Are they not guaranteed victory?"

Disease, as a weapon of war. Germs replacing bombs, grenades, rifles, missiles, and other modern means of shedding blood in the course of waging war. And vastly more deadly.

"And if it works," Cyril pointed out, "someday, perhaps a century or two from now, Islamic foes could use the same technique against them. Annihilation of whole countries could become part of a diabolical cycle. How demonic!"

Taking turns driving, the two men rode in silence the rest of the day, visions of ancient pestilence robbing them of words.

CHAPTER 2

Just over a day later. . .

The two men made it to the outskirts of Cherbourg. Just a few miles from the harbor area, Alberto Liberatore brought the old Fiat to a halt on a dirt road.

"Why are you stopping here?" Cyril asked.

"I cannot go on to Great Britain with you, Lord Fothergill," Liberatore reluctantly told him, announcing a decision that was far from an easy one for him.

"But you will not be safe anywhere in Italy. You're undoubtedly a marked man."

"Gervasio's influence spreads beyond the boundaries of one country."

"Then it is likely that the farther away you are, the safer you will be."

"That is true."

"Reconsider, I beg you. Edling will find whatever you can tell him illuminating."

"But then we are back where we started, without the support of His Holiness, and no clearing of your name, Lord Fothergill."

What Alberto Liberatore was saying seemed unassailable, and Cyril gave up trying to rebut his arguments.

"How will you survive the new scrutiny that will be heaped upon you?" he asked, deeply concerned.

"I could concoct some reasonable-sounding story that would satisfy Gervasio for the time being," Liberatore declared. "He is accustomed to me telling the truth. His weakness may be that that is all he expects of me. It seems curious that he respects someone who is honorable in the face of his own corruption."

Lying. . .

To do that would mean engaging in an act of outright falsehood, and Cyril was nervous about this, well aware that lying was forbidden by Scripture. But he also recognized the nature of the foul little man with whom they were dealing.

"If you fail to do that," he reasoned, "if Gervasio should realize or even suspect where your sympathies are, that devil would get rid of you as quickly as he disposed of Dante Fratto and Eduardo Pintozzi and, now, Geoffrey Cowlishaw."

Another death.

Three good men slaughtered by someone who could not behave as he was without some pact with the source of all evil.

"And there I would be, headed for safety in England, while you might be dying as a thousand rats poured over your flesh?" Cyril continued. "Do you think I could cope with that for the rest of my life? Do you think I could look at my reflection in a mirror and not find myself thoroughly repugnant?"

Liberatore was equally perplexed by the dilemma that both of them faced.

"But how can I answer Monsignor Gervasio directly, and yet do so without at least a measure of subterfuge?" he asked.

"You suggest that he will confront you in a way that would demand the truth, or that he would confront you at all. He might not, you know. He might be too busy sending out men to track me down without realizing what you did, making sure that everything is in place so that Adolfo will accept his version of what happened."

"I have to assume that he overlooks few details," Liberatore said. "When I am missed for a period of days, but suddenly show up again of my own accord, he will insist upon learning what happened."

Cyril thought for a moment, the common sense of what had just been said hard to debate.

"Here is an idea then," he suggested. "But it does require some fresh pain on your part, as well as mine."

"If some pain is all that I have to face over the coming days and weeks, I shall consider myself fortunate."

"You must cut yourself on your neck, your legs, elsewhere. Make sure you are sufficiently bloodied to be believable when you tell Gervasio, should he actually ask, that I escaped. The way you look will indicate some kind of struggle. What he assumes from this is his, not your lie."

Liberatore was uncomfortable with that.

"But what if he does ask about a fight between us?"

"We shall have had one then."

"I could not hurt a man such as you," Liberatore confessed. "Every part of me that cries out, 'Christian! Christian!' forbids it."

Cyril swung out with his right fist and knocked the other man on the ground.

"If it means your survival, you will have to!" he exclaimed. "And you must not forget that there is also the matter of the survival of Europe itself."

Liberatore jumped to his feet and grabbed Cyril, hitting him hard in the stomach.

And then he stood in the middle of the dirt road and wept.

"To fight the wicked, that is most honorable!" Liberatore cried. "But to hurt a good man is folly."

"It is my turn now!" Cyril remarked.

"I have been trained all my adult life to defend myself and others, to fight back. I would instinctively do so now."

"Good! I was hoping that would be the case."

"This is barbaric."

"But necessary!" Cyril told him emphatically. "You must look sufficiently beaten for Gervasio to assume that I escaped by subduing you."

He paused, looking at the other man.

"You could do something else," he suggested. "Fighting me is not the only choice that you could make."

"What then?" Liberatore asked.

"You could go on with me after all. You could leave everything at the Vatican purely in God's hands."

Liberatore bit his lower lip as he carefully chose his words.

"I feel that I would be doing nothing more than running

away if I went with you, Lord Fothergill."

"And what about the sovereignty of our Creator? Are you not trying to outthink Him?"

"But you overlook the fact that he often uses human instruments to do His will. I might be the only one available."

"But what changed your mind?" Cyril was not eager to embark alone upon a journey such as the one ahead of him, memories of the last one not yet dissipated.

"At first I did not think that way but during the past few hours, I have arrived at that conclusion. I must return to St. Peter's," Liberatore explained, "to become a force for reform."

"But both Fratto and Pintozzi acknowledged that, as 'lowly' Vatican guards, they had no real influence."

"My comrades were right, Lord Fothergill. Only the elite closest to Adolfo do, and with Gervasio around, even those are being shunted aside, sometimes unceremoniously."

Liberatore lowered his voice and spoke as though ears other than theirs could hear what he was saying.

"I have heard of a conspiracy. . . ."

He was testing the waters as he spoke, not wanting to appear to know so much that Cyril would become suspicious.

"It seems that they too are disgusted," Liberatore continued. "They see the deception, the excesses, the rest of it, and their nostrils are filled with the same stench that I smell, a stench that intensifies daily."

"I have heard of such a conspiracy," Cyril remarked. "From what I can gather, Gervasio's severest critics are behind it, waiting for the right moment to entrap him.

"But I have the impression that none of them is well organized, and that there are some competing voices threatening to stymie the whole thing."

"I know the men involved," Liberatore assured him. "They do not play the role of fools."

"But are they wise enough to do it right?" Cyril asked. "Are these men you know actually capable of the sort of warped thinking that will be necessary to counteract Gervasio's own perversities?"

Liberatore paled, then asked, "Could it be that Baldasarre Gervasio is so evil that we have to wonder if there is anyone who can match him without being more foul and demonic than he?"

Cyril loathed any such thought, any notion that, to fight a man who was devilish, some of his own techniques had to be turned against him if there were any hope of bringing about his downfall.

"You are uncomfortable?" Liberatore observed.

"Yes, I am. I feel almost that anyone attempting to get rid of Gervasio must give up some of his Christianity in order to succeed. That in itself is a hellish thought."

"Nor would I be at peace doing what you imply."

"Then what hope is there?"

"I did not say that I would let this stop me."

Liberatore was shuffling his oversized feet as he stood beside the Fiat.

"I have access to every inch of the basilica," he boasted, "as well as every piece of furniture within it. And I also know about all the secret places."

"*Secret* places?"

Cyril's pulse was quickening.

"Rooms behind walls? That sort of thing? Is this what you are suggesting?"

"Yes! Gervasio must be keeping records of whatever sort. I doubt that everything can be in his mind."

Cyril was becoming more intrigued.

"If I can find these bits and pieces," Liberatore added, "and decipher them, and there is anything at all incriminating, I can go directly to the holy father."

He struck an ironic tone in his voice.

"One advantage of being taken for granted, of being part of the woodwork, I suppose, is that I would seem to have a clean slate," he continued. "Even Gervasio could not reasonably accuse me of having an axe to grind, as they say. He has no idea where I stand!

"Frankly, I have never gone on record here or anywhere

else about anything of controversy or importance. Even in the more impetuous days of my youth, I have kept silent, and have been accused by my peers of not having substance, of being vapid."

A mischievous smile crossed his face.

"But then it is also quite true that I have done or said nothing that could hurt my case either."

The man seemed like a little boy ready to trick or bluff as many of the adults around him as he could.

Cyril sensed how he felt.

"I think you may be right to remain," he acknowledged. "That is easy for me to say since I soon shall be leaving danger while you will be walking back into its midst. But then, you probably could not accomplish with Edling what I have a slim chance at, and I could not hope to do what you might. It is beginning to look as though God has placed us squarely where He wants us."

"For one thing," Liberatore went on, "I can visit with Pope Adolfo anytime I want simply because I have never abused the privilege of being able to talk with him privately about matters that are on my heart and my soul."

Cyril was beginning to feel more hopeful.

"How influential are the men from whom you could receive cooperation, within St. Peter's and elsewhere?" he asked, aware that one member of the Vatican guard alone could not achieve what was needed.

"Certainly less than what they once were but not at the point of being completely emasculated either."

"Would they act for the good of the church or for their own self-interests?"

"Does it matter?"

That question caught Cyril by surprise. He thought he knew the answer without thinking about it but he considered it further.

"If the end result is the same, if it is a victory for the kingdom of God," he pondered, "do the means matter?"

"It is an awful notion, I know," Liberatore agreed, "hardly

the stuff of old-fashioned Christian integrity. The apostles would have fought against anything of the sort."

Cyril could not disagree.

"So awful, as you say, my brother, that I have no alternative but to leave the result in God's hands, and turn my guilt over to Him."

"We make a mess of our affairs and expect Him to come in and clean it up."

Cyril nodded unhappily.

"Be on the alert," he cautioned urgently. "And know that I will pray for you daily."

"And I will pray for you as well, Lord Fothergill."

"No longer 'Lord.' We rightly have but one Lord between us. Call me Cyril, dear brother, no more than that."

"And you may call me—"

Abruptly Liberatore turned away, his shoulders slumped. When he faced Cyril again, his cheeks were wet.

"Call me Alberto," he said, his voice cracking. "If our God be just and merciful, as we both know Him to be without fail, you and I will meet again."

"Oh, we will. . .we will. . .should righteousness stand."

"May it ever!"

They gripped each other's hands in silence.

"Losing Geoffrey. . ." Cyril started to mutter, "that way . . .any way."

"I understand," Liberatore told him. "I saw what was left of him, you know, a horrible pile of—"

"Tell me. I must hear."

Desperation was written on Cyril's face.

"You should not know, Lord. . .Cyril," Liberatore said. "Trust me when I say that you should never know."

"But my imagination will conjure up bloody images anyway. What could the difference be?"

"Anything is better than what I saw. . . ."

Liberatore was struggling to control himself.

"After some of my comrades and I disposed of the remains, I happened to overhear what Gervasio was planning regarding your fate. That was why I went looking for you. I could not let his trap spring shut."

"How did you know where to find me?"

"I know his mind after spending two years with him. I knew he would want you where you would be at a terrible disadvantage. He spends so much time in the catacombs. It seemed appropriate for someone of his ilk."

"But is that not strange enough in itself to make at least a few people wonder what is going on?" Cyril asked.

"Some say that he is merely an archaeologist at heart. Others say that they, too, have retreated on occasion to the utter isolation of the catacombs. The difference is that no one dares to ask Gervasio why."

Liberatore was markedly uncomfortable. "Even the holy father ignores this, allowing the man his eccentricities. That is a devilish word, you know, eccentricities. It lets the wicked get away with so much."

He stepped away, his face pale.

"Just as I was heading through the main entrance, I came face-to-face with Gervasio, who was leaving. At first he seemed somewhat startled, for he was not prepared to find me there, then he smiled in that crooked way of his and remarked cryptically, 'Our sins have been washed away. We need not be bothered again.' He saw that I was puzzled, and added, 'It is of no concern to you, Alberto, none at all. The Lord deals with the wicked as He sees fit, and we must rejoice in that.'"

"So you assumed that he was talking about me."

"And somehow I suspected right away what Gervasio meant when he spoke of sins being washed away, hardly a statement of biblical doctrine in this case, I was sure. So, I decided to investigate every inch of the Tiber, at the rear of the basilica. I found you not very long afterward."

"But surely you had to have some other clue," Cyril suggested. "Just those few words seem hardly enough."

"But you have not been the first he disposed of in that manner," Liberatore recalled. "I put those two matters together, and it turned out I was right. In many ways, Gervasio is very predictable."

"I owe my life to you."

Liberatore nodded.

"I am but our Heavenly Father's humble and imperfect instrument," he replied contritely, "nothing more."

"And nothing less," Cyril told him.

They kissed one another on each cheek in the European manner.

"You seem Italian," the member of the Vatican guard said with great warmth.

"And you have a bit of Britain in you," Cyril replied.

At that Liberatore strode back to the compact vehicle. His hands on the steering wheel, he announced, "I think I am doing the right thing by leaving you, but I cannot be sure. Nor do I have total peace about this."

While Liberatore dawdled for a few seconds, Cyril felt great empathy for the man, thinking that Alberto might throw away all that he had said about remaining within the Vatican and, after all, board a ship for England.

You have to go, good fellow, Cyril thought. *You were right in what you said. I understand your feelings, and shall do nothing to try and change them, if that is what you are wanting.*

Cyril spoke up, mustering a smile that he did not feel and a hopefulness to his voice that seemed forced.

"I will pray for you unrelentingly, Alberto."

"And I for you, my brother."

Cyril waved good-bye as Alberto Liberatore, noticeably sighing, turned on the ignition and started back along the dirt road, commencing again the long journey that led east across the upper part of France and, ultimately, due south to Italy.

"Please be with him, dear Heavenly Father," Cyril whispered, the first of many prayers for his companion. "Be with Alberto every step he takes."

No prayer had he ever spoken more earnestly.

Before seeking out a captain and ship, Cyril Fothergill

*decided to pay Henry Letchworth a visit. He had thought
often of Henry and, judging by Henry's actions and the few
times he had spoken, wondered how serious his so-called im-
pairment really was, not knowing how much more he would
ques-tion over the coming days. . .*

It took him no more than a few minutes to find the tiny
residence after having the good fortune of approaching someone who told him exactly where to turn.

Two candles were flickering in the single small front
window.

Cyril walked slowly up the pathway to the front door,
knowing now he would not turn and walk away. He tapped
a fist against the door. Immediately he heard plodding footsteps inside.

"Please come in," Henry said pleasantly after recogniz-
ing him. "It has been only days, I know, since I saw you at
my brother's funeral. Most of Cherbourg was there, even
Frenchmen who have hated the British for centuries."

Beneath the welcoming facade, Cyril noted that the other
man seemed quite sad.

"You appear to have quite a weight on your shoulders,"
he remarked.

"It is a sad world, Lord Fothergill," Henry replied. "There
is little joy in life, if we are honest with ourselves. We live,
we die, and in between, we have scattered moments of comfort and pleasure. There is little more to life than that."

When Geoffrey and he were on Maximilian Letchworth's ship, they both had noted Henry's somber manner.

"But then how would you or I react if either of us were
in his circumstances instead of who we are and what we
have?" Geoffrey had commented. "We have all our faculties,
certainly. I doubt that we have ever been desperate about anything, not food, not clothes, not a roof over our heads, not
money, especially not money. And, of course, no one would
dare to mumble things about us behind our backs."

"I wish we could help him in some way," Cyril had
acknowledged. "He will be able to get by as long as he has

his brother with him. But if anything were to happen to the captain, how would Henry cope?"

They had debated the possibility of bringing Henry to England and trying to get him some more education.

"We could divide the cost between us," Geoffrey suggested.

"And I have many rooms that are never occupied. My castle was planned generations ago for a large family. Having Henry stay there would not be a burden at all."

"He needs to feel some self-respect. I doubt that he would respond well to pure charity. He could work for you or for me. Even if neither of us had any position open, it could be created just for Henry!"

Thinking of Geoffrey, his face animated, brought Cyril up against a reality that was like a sudden fist to his jaw.

I could not even say goodbye, he thought. *And I may never know where they put whatever was left of his—*

He felt weak and his head was throbbing.

Henry became concerned.

"Lord Fothergill," he asked, "is there anything I can do?"

"No, there is nothing. But I am grateful that you thought to ask. I have been through a great deal. I need some rest. After that, I should feel better."

"Why not sit by the fire?" Henry asked. "You can tell me whatever you want there. Maximilian and I used to do that after he returned from his sea voyages with enthralling tales to tell."

They spent a number of hours talking and remembering, interrupted only by a plain but filling dinner of lamb and muffins. Cyril decided to try and convince Henry to make the trip to England with him, arguing that, with his brother gone, he had no remaining ties in Cherbourg or elsewhere, for that matter. Surprisingly, Henry offered no resistance but agreed to accompany his new friend. He also proved instrumental in finding another vessel that would take them across the English Channel, a journey that would end as neither of them dared to anticipate. . . .

CHAPTER 3

Cyril placed a short call to his family, admitting that he should have done so long before. He did not tell his loved ones anything but the barest outline of what had happened since his departure, omitting the horrific details.

Elizabeth, Clarice, and Sarah told him that he had been in their prayers.

"That is why I am able to return to you," he said.

He would call again but not until another part of the drama of his odyssey had been played out, with yet more danger ahead, for they were less than a third of the way across the English Channel when the storm hit.

It came upon them in a rush, dark clouds appearing at a faster rate than any of those veteran seafarers could remember: the sky darkening; wind blowing with a ferocity that seemed to make of itself a prowling beast of the night, invisible but ferocious, ready to consume; the temperature dropping; waves starting to rise up from what had been a routinely placid surface.

"Some of the men are talking strangely," Henry alerted Cyril as they stood below deck in the little hallway outside the only passenger cabin on the ship.

"This is enough of a storm to terrify anyone!" Cyril declared, his eyes widening. "I can scarcely blame any of those blokes."

"It is far, far more serious than that," Henry added. "They are talking about the presence of demons, demons whose foul images they spotted for a second or two, and then were gone!"

"I do not think Gervasio has that kind of power," Cyril said as he leaned against the wall. "Certainly not this far away from where he holds court."

"But, Cyril, to whom does this Gervasio pledge his allegiance?" Henry asked pointedly.

"Satan, of course. . . ."

Cyril's voice trailed off as he got the other man's point.

"All he has to do is pass the word," Henry offered.

"And demons do their master's bidding."

"You must not be allowed to return alive, Cyril. You now know everything. Convincing others is a task that you will have to face, and not one most other men could handle.

"But as long as you are safe, as long as the prime minister's power attempts to protect you on home soil, there is a chance that someone will listen and act before it is too late."

Cyril quickly pointed out the worst part, the part that Henry had left unsaid.

"Which means that by being here," he said, "I shall be taking all of you with me when the end comes, though no one else has any direct involvement in these matters."

Henry did not consider that possibility to be very likely.

"By the grace of God, the crewmates and I will be safe, my brother," he commented confidently. "And after this voyage is completed, the group of us go will back to our homes and continue on with our lives as before, with another crossing a month from now, and another after that. Our way of life stands."

Henry paused, then slowed his speech, its very pace ominous.

"But for you," he intoned, "there may be an unending series of battles to be fought for the rest of your life. You will never be free of what has started!"

Cyril's pulse quickened.

"And I will never know who will be perhaps the latest emissary intending to do me harm," he stated anxiously. "This can only lead me to examining strangers with a hostility that most would not deserve.

"But how could I avoid that, Henry? Any enemy of mine would not have signs hanging from his shoulders, proclaiming his allegiance to Satan! Only men and women I have known for a long time could be trusted."

"Not always," Henry noted. "People can become thoroughly corrupted."

Cyril thought of Elizabeth, Clarice, and Sarah.

Clarice seems strong, he told himself, *and so does Elizabeth, but my dear Sarah, what about her? She is strong of spirit but her body is weak.*

"And your family, Cyril," Henry continued, as though reading his thoughts. "Every member of your family will be at risk, you know."

He seemed to be more and more melancholy.

"I have no one, you see," he said. "Maximilian is gone. That house, as small as it is, will seem oppressive now, empty when I return to it each time, a tomb that claims me briefly and then spits me out for yet another voyage."

Henry closed his eyes, focusing on a vision that was certain to be repeated often over the coming weeks and months as the grief cycle played out.

He sighed. "Where should I make my home? Should I stay there, always close to the harbor, Cyril, and be surrounded by the old things, squeezing some comfort from them? Or should I go elsewhere? Should I build something new for myself, if I have the energy left to do so? What about England? It seems a fine place, not as beautiful as Switzerland, but hardly flat and uninteresting."

Cyril never got to answer.

Suddenly the ship seemed to be lifted up, then smashed down hard, and the two men were knocked off their feet. And then there was a sound like of that of thousands of demons shrieking in the wind. Cyril froze for an instant, his experiences at the Vatican too fresh to be ignored, any hint of supernatural intervention a red flag before him.

Have I been followed? he thought. *There may be no rats this time but taking their place might be something infinitely more terrifying!*

He shook his head and continued up the steps, Henry just ahead of him. They both made it to the deck, near the bow, but with the advantage of railings on both sides to steady themselves, something denied the crew members. Even so, it was an ordeal to keep moving, as rocking, twisting motions took hold of the ship, and water pouring down those steps made them slippery.

"God in heaven!" Henry gasped.

Crewmen were sprawled across the battered surface of the old wooden deck, looking like helpless doll-like figures. The ones not knocked unconscious were trying to get to their feet, most without success.

One mate managed to stagger over to Henry.

"This is an evil storm!" he exclaimed, his face lashed by wind and rain. "I think we are being played with by something unholy. Satan himself may be attacking. And there is no priest around! We are doomed."

Henry tried to calm him but the man backed away, toward the stern of the ship. He was beyond panic and seemed to be on the edge of madness.

Cyril was clutching the railing on that side as he glanced out at the English Channel.

"Dear God!" he cried out. "Help us!"

"What is it?" Henry asked.

"There! A whirlpool!"

Henry squinted through what was essentially zero visibility. And then he saw it, that dreaded swirling mass of water, with a funnel-shaped hole in the center, like a tornado displaced to the sea instead of land.

"I cannot control the ship any longer!" the navigator yelled pitiably, trying to steer away from it. "She is being drawn toward that—!"

The storm was so violent that he had lost all control of the ship, the elements taking over mercilessly. Strong men were now being flung from one side of the vessel to another, mumbling like scared children, not strictly because of the storm, for they had been through many over the years, but what they perceived about this storm, the hint of something supernatural out in the darkness surrounding them; that was what stripped away their valor and reduced them to what they had become.

"We will die!" someone screamed. "Hell's fury is going

to squash us like—"

That shrill, terrified voice was snuffed out as a giant wave hit his chest and knocked him over the edge of the ship.

His mates followed him, kicking wildly, reaching out to grab something, but failing, unable to resist the might of that raging storm, which seemed maniacal in its fury. Within less than two minutes they were gone. Not one crew member remained.

Dead. All of them.

Cyril saw several of the bodies, stark expressions of terror frozen on their lifeless faces as they floated past his vision one by one until they sank beneath the surface.

Instinctively he tried to tighten his grip on the railing. His hands! They would not move.

*Oh, Lord, Lord, they—! * he exclaimed to himself. *I can feel nothing. They are completely—*

Both hands had become numb from the cold rain, sleet-like as it was.

I cannot let go, he thought. *Somehow I cannot let go.*

As his eyes searched the now empty deck, from bow to stern, Cyril was aware of one obvious but unnerving fact.

He was alone.

"Oh, Jesus, Jesus!" he muttered prayerfully out loud, as frightened now as he had been in the catacombs of St. Peter's, perhaps more so since he seemed even less in control.

Henry and he had to carry on the battle alone, their bodies tired, strength ebbing, and drenched with water that felt like liquid ice.

At that moment the ship was entering the whirlpool. And there was no one at the helm!

The bow of the ship was being pulled down, sucked into the whirlpool's maw.

Cyril and Henry began sliding forward, their individual grips on the railing wrenched free, with nothing else available that they could grab hold of.

"You and I are being emptied out of the ship like sugar from a cup!" Cyril yelled.

Around the vessel was going, the two men helpless in their encompassing dizziness, wobbly legs unable to keep them standing.

Cyril's head hit the deck hard and he nearly passed out.

"I will hold you!" Henry called to him most urgently. "We will die together, the two of us, a Fothergill and a Letchworth, if we die at all this night. . .and there we will be, walking past the gates of heaven at the very same time!

"Nothing the devil can fling at us can separate you and me, now or for eternity! Take hold of that, my brother, and let it give you what little peace is possible in the midst of this maddening fury that seems to be from the pit of hell!"

Cyril felt Henry's strong grip on his arm.

"My wife, my daughters!" he screamed hoarsely. "They will never know what happened to me. And the plague! It will—"

They first heard, then saw, the mast break, splitting in the middle, plummeting toward them, unable to hold up under the force of the whirlpool and the storm.

They were flung from the deck, tossed into the rioting sea by a ship that was to perish without a single human being onboard after a decade of having them for company, reduced ruthlessly to bits and pieces of itself floating on currents for miles in every direction.

The heavy mast was thicker at the point they were clinging to it, and they were in no danger of making it sink because of their combined weight. But then, drowning was not the major problem they faced.

Cold and shivering, both men were more worried about dying from exposure than any terror of the sea.

"If this were winter. . ." Henry began.

"We would be dead by now," Cyril finished.

"Is there some Providence in that?"

"I would think so, Henry."

And then both men blacked out.

More than an hour passed, a time in which both men went

in and out of consciousness, though nothing caused them to loosen their death grip on the mast.

Morning came, the storm passing. Sunrise cast brightness over water that was visibly beginning to calm down.

Squinting, Cyril noticed some misty shapes in the distance.

"The white cliffs. . ." he said weakly.

Henry was silent momentarily, longing for an end to the nightmare, then gasped.

"What is it?" Cyril asked.

"Look. . . ."

Cyril turned toward where the other man was pointing. Fins.

"*Lord help us!*" he exclaimed.

Five of them. About 600 feet away. And coming nearer.

Suddenly, the sun broke through some clouds.

"You were right!" it was Henry's turn to exclaim.

"Right? About—"

The white cliffs of Dover loomed up ahead, about half a mile away, offering refuge. . .a symbol of the ageless stability that once had been embodied throughout the British Empire.

But now the sharks were even closer than before.

"We will have to swim," Cyril said, already judging the distance to the shore.

"You and I could have done that yesterday, before the storm howled," Henry told him. "But now we are too tired, weak, cold, hungry. We will never make it."

He spoke as a man of the sea.

"The sharks would get to us long before we could make it to shore," he said.

Nevertheless, he seemed undaunted.

"I have noticed that they do not swim side by side," he mused. "They are almost always in single file."

His expression brightened as he thought for a moment, and added, "As soon as the first one approaches—"

"We could ram it with the mast," Cyril said, clearly in

tune with his friend.

They both nodded, glad that they did not have to submit themselves to the predators without a fight. But that first shark was just one of five. And once blood was shed, others would be drawn to the scene. All Cyril and Henry could hope to achieve was a delay, perhaps time enough to be spotted from shore or by a crew member from another ship emerging in the vicinity.

Just a fewscore feet away now, that first shark, probably the leader of the pack, was heading toward them at a right angle. If they combined what little strength they each had left, they might be able to give the mast a sudden stabbing motion —they would have but one opportunity to do this, and to do it perfectly—and jam the heavy wood through the shark's partially open jaws and down its throat as far as they could.

The shark was nearly at the opposite end of the mast.

"Now!" Henry said.

With a steadiness and an accuracy that they would have thought impossible minutes before, they propelled the wooden mast into the shark's mouth, rapidly jamming it farther and farther down. By the time they had to stop, they were only two or three feet from the shark's snout, close enough to see the teeth of this creature, and to smell an odor coming from within that reeked of decay. It finally snapped the mast off in two at that point. The remaining section was not more than seven-and-a-quarter-feet long.

Cyril and Henry frantically clung to it as they saw that one shark opening and closing its jaws in pain-ridden motions, as it swam erratically away from them, first to the left, then the right, until it started sinking, the mast jutting a number of inches out of its mouth.

"Four to go!" Henry said, with a surge of optimism that bordered on the childlike.

"Better count again," Cyril told him, pointing just to the left of the shark they had killed.

Not just four fins. Half a dozen more were swimming toward them, like torpedoes ready to hit their targets.

"We will die now!" Henry exclaimed, trying to be stoic but failing as tears left his eyes and trickled down his cheeks. "We will disappear, you know, the sea swallowing us up as it has done with so many before you and I were ever born."

He clutched Cyril's hand, seized of a special passion that ardent faith had lent him.

"Into the kingdom together!" he proclaimed, a bright, brave smile on his face.

Cyril was silent, his heart beating faster, as his gaze fixed on something else.

There straight ahead was another group of fins, these black and white instead of gray, larger by half than any fins belonging to the sharks.

For more minutes than Cyril and Henry could calculate, the salt water around them was being churned as though another storm had broken out. The sharks made no sounds whatever, but the whales were emitting a variety of different ones, seemingly calling to one another, which did not surprise either man since their encounter with the mother whale and her baby.

The sharks, while tough from years of experience as saltwater marauders, were no match for the far bigger, heavier creatures. After their initial resistance, three were killed instantly, two of them cut to pieces, the remaining ones swimming away at such a fast pace that their movement seemed almost comical. That section of the English Channel near shore was strewn with what was left of the three dead sharks, bits and pieces of them floating for a while, then sinking where scavengers below the surface of the water would get a meal.

"They would have stayed if there had been only one adult whale and a little one," Henry muttered with contempt. "They are worse cowards than some of the men poor Maximilian had as crew members some few years ago."

"Or they saw the odds, and simply retreated," Cyril suggested.

What was left was no less extraordinary a sight: all seven whales choosing to remain briefly, still grouped more or less in a circle around the two frail human beings yet clinging to less than eight feet of a ship's mast.

And then, one by one, the huge sea mammals swam away, having done what they set out to do and now it was time to go on elsewhere. Except for two.

"What are *they* waiting for?" Cyril asked, not really expecting that Henry would know the answer, but needing to say something because what they had witnessed was yet another chapter in what he was beginning to think of as more than just a coincidental series of events.

Now that it should have been time for the two whales to leave, having accomplished what they apparently wanted, that was not what they were doing.

Cyril shivered as he considered what Henry had said.

Lord, how could this be? he thought. *We need Your help. What should we do? We can hardly wait for these creatures, however wonderful they are, to act first.*

Swim. That word rose in his mind.

"Swim. . ." he said out loud, without hesitating.

"I am weaker now than before, and colder, and you ask me to swim to shore?" Henry reminded him. "How can we—?

"We have no choice, do we?" he spoke, seeing Cyril's expression, and certain that the other man had arrived at the same conclusion.

"None," Cyril replied.

Slowly, tentatively, both let go of that remaining portion of a mast that had been on its ship for more than twenty years. As they started to swim, Cyril and Henry became alarmed at what little strength was left in their arms and their legs.

"I cannot make it, I—" Henry pleaded pitiably, "I shall sink to my death."

His limbs were numb, and moving them even slightly was unendurably painful.

Cyril paddled close to him, putting his left arm around the man's waist.

"Hold onto me!" Cyril begged him. "We might survive if we do this together."

"*No!*" Henry said.

"We have nothing else. We must—"

"This cannot be!" Henry protested. "You will sink as well, Cyril. You may be stronger than me. . .I. . .I think you are. . .but not enough to take over for both of us.

"Go on ahead, my brother, do not sacrifice yourself. You have too much to tell the prime minister, valuable information he needs to know! As for me, I can die and be missed by no one."

"I will *not* desert you!" Cyril declared. "If we die, we die right now, you and I, and we do it *together,* but then we awaken together to your brother's presence in—"

Henry's eyes widened at the scene his mind conjured up.

"You speak honestly, Cyril, you speak the truth. My brother, yes. . .waiting. . .oh, how I yearn to tell him such a great deal. How I yearn to hold him again, and know that we will never again be separated."

"Move your arms, Henry, help me."

Henry tried but could not budge them.

"Paralyzed, Cyril! I command them, and they refuse to obey me. They—"

Cyril was not going to be defeated, knowing that their survival could be had but a few hundred feet away.

"Then I shall do it for both of us!" Cyril declared with just a little pomposity. "God give me the strength!"

On shore, a crowd had gathered, about a dozen men and some women and children watching. Five of the adults, now alerted to how desperate the strangers' situation had become, were wading into the water, and swimming frantically toward them.

Too great a distance. . .

But however altruistically they were acting, the would-be rescuers were kidding themselves. The tide was now going out and there was an undertow, a combination that would defeat the efforts of all but the strongest men.

Henry's considerable weight and his own extreme weakness were a hopeless combination.

"The undertow's pulling me down!" Henry screamed. "I . . .I am not able to—"

Henry knew how to swim well but he was becoming confused, the limits on his mind impairing his judgment, and he started to move away from Cyril who could not reach him in time as Henry sank below the surface.

Then something rubbery but also hard and smooth touched him. One of the whales, unnoticed, had dived underwater and started back up again directly under Henry's body. With astonishing gentleness and precision, it lifted him up as it broke majestically through the surface of the water.

"Grab its fin!" Cyril shouted as he saw that awesome sight burst forth, a man balanced uncertainly on the back of a one-and-a-half-ton, jet-black, snow-white killer whale. "Grab—"

But Henry could not catch it in time. A look of terror distorting his face, he slipped off the whale and disappeared.

"*Oh, God, oh, God!*" Cyril repeated prayerfully.

At that instant the whale dived yet again. Then it showed up the second time with Henry once more straddling its back. This time he had managed to wrap his arms partway around that imposing fin, taller and wider than he was, and was holding on as tightly as he could manage, even if this meant some pain for the whale as his fingers dug into its skin.

Suddenly panicking, and ashamed of himself for it, Cyril realized that while Henry was being helped, he himself seemed to have been left behind, and was still being forced to swim toward shore on his own dwindling reservoir of strength. His arms and legs. . .he began to have the same difficulty moving his limbs that Henry had experienced.

I may never see you again, Elizabeth, Cyril thought. *If I do not make it, I hope our Lord Jesus finds some way to tell you how much I have loved you all the years of our life together.*

Cyril then looked around for the other whale but it was gone, and he felt helplessly alone.

Something touched his feet briefly, then his legs, and

he had the terrifying sensation of being lifted up quite unexpectedly by a huge black mass.

The second whale had *not* left. It had simply hovered out of sight somewhere beneath his body, seemingly waiting until—

Cyril did what he had asked Henry to do.

Slippery. The fin was slippery.

Cyril understood why Henry had had so much difficulty because he, too, was starting to slide down and off the whale's back.

"No!" he declared out loud. "I will not die this morning, Heavenly Father. I will ride this wonderful creature You have provided, and I *will* survive!"

Cyril pressed his feet into the whale's side much like he would when he rode a horse bareback on his estate, and *climbed* toward the fin, coming within reach in seconds. He grabbed hold of it so hard that his fingers punctured the flesh but the whale gave no indication that this had caused it any distress. A sudden wind from the east was bracing as it swept across his face and Henry's. The few human would-be rescuers had returned hastily to shore, not eager to be in the path of two large killer whales.

"We *will* make it!" Henry called out expectantly. "By the mercy of God we will make it!"

Cyril heard him, and might have branded the other man as far too optimistic except for the intoxicating surge of emotion he also felt while riding the back of a whale toward shore, an exhilarating sensation he had never known before pounding at his temples. But something else was becoming clear to him. Cyril now had little doubt that Henry and he would survive, a possibility that seemed beyond any hope just a short while before, and he rejoiced in this. Except for that which he knew was inevitable.

Dear Father, he prayed silently, *I understand that it has to be but how tragic for these extraordinary creatures.*

To get close enough, the two whales would have to beach themselves.

They cannot know this, Cyril thought. *How could what they are doing be any kind of conscious act of sacrifice?*

He hugged the fin more tightly, his tears mixing with the salt water lashing against his face. The whale carrying Henry was first on the beach, its mammoth body thumping against the sand, immediately trying to dislodge itself even as Henry slid off, while two men waded in and carried him the rest of the way. It thrashed about in a desperate frenzy, able to move a few inches backward but no more. After a short while, it had exhausted itself. And then came the whale on which Cyril rode, the larger of the two. It hit the sand harder, and emitted what seemed to be a whimpering sound.

Cyril jumped off and, after stumbling a yard or two, was helped by the same men.

"Look!" one woman shouted.

The larger whale was agonizingly inching its way over to the smaller one and came very close, but collapsed without making the remaining few feet.

"What is—?" someone yelled from the crowd of two dozen that had gathered.

A sound arose not like any that they had heard before then.

The two beached whales seemed to be calling out, perhaps to others of their kind or in simple, awful pain. It may have been that they were, in their own way, pleading for mercy. Several of the children clamped hands over their ears. The men just stood and looked, trying not to show any emotion. And then, after a short while, it ended, and the whales became quite still, as though they were already dead.

"Thank God *that's* over with!" a man named Derek Freemantle said as he introduced himself to Cyril and Henry. "We have very humble dwellings around here but we offer you whatever hospitality we can. You both need something to eat. My wife will fix some porridge and a pot of tea. Come on, gents, let's—"

The sound of horses interrupted him. And then a booming voice proclaimed, "No need, people, no need. My doctors will take care of them!"

An elaborate carriage, jet-black and edged in gold with large wheels, pulled up to the edge of a promontory rising over a dozen feet above that part of the beach. Immediately a small man, dressed in the elegant and dated clothes that would have suited a king of several generations earlier, stood up and faced them, his expression stern, as he surveyed the scene.

"Lord Selwyn," Freemantle acknowledged, his voice cold.

One of the wealthiest men in England, Selwyn had become also one of the more isolated, and decidedly eccentric —and perhaps the most mysterious as a result. He continued to dress in the manner of medieval English nobility, preferring carriages to automobiles. While other men in his class tended to travel considerably, using their wealth to spend time on the continent or perhaps in Africa, Nigel Selwyn assumed the role of a hermit or a monk, coming out only on the rarest occasions, and insisting that his guards dress as knights and describe themselves that way, avoiding any comparison with their modern-day counterparts.

"Your offer is appreciated," Selwyn continued, "but I can provide these two men more of the proper care they need than, I daresay, any of you people can afford. They need the best medicine, they need the finest food, and they need rest in comfortable beds."

Already the little man, and that he was, all four feet, nine inches of him, had sent servants down to the beach.

Glancing a bit furtively at Selwyn who looked quite odd, dressed as he was in modern England, Cyril looked apologetically at Freemantle.

"This chap may be right," he said, almost embarrassed, but knowing Selwyn had spoken accurately.

"Now I see, I surely do," Freemantle said cynically.

"What do you mean?" Cyril asked.

"The rich have the most to offer, and the poor must step aside or be left in their wake."

Henry was being helped to his feet.

"Wait a minute!" he protested with striking vigor. "I have

been poor. And I would become poor again if I ever lost my work. I have no savings. I lived until recently in a tiny house with my brother."

"Did he kick you out?" Freemantle spat those words from his mouth with undisguised cynicism, detecting by the sound of the other man's voice and the way he seemed to be forcing some of his words out that Henry was not as "sharp" as some men.

But Henry was emboldened, intent on not letting Freemantle's sarcasm pass by unchallenged.

"No, he died. He was killed at sea."

Henry was wobbly as he walked up to the other man.

"True kindness is not something that comes from the poor and them alone," he said, nose to nose with Freemantle. "The poor *can* be brutally cruel at times, homeless women dumping their babies in the Thames, and walking away with nary a tear; husbands beating their wives; and much else that you know of as well as I, unless you are incapable of admitting truths apparent to every man here.

"It is the *love* of money and the improper *use* of it that corrupts a man, if he allows this to happen. A beggar can take a coin given to him by a sympathetic bystander and purchase more whiskey, yet a lord who has been blessed with much land and other holdings may elect to spend many times that amount to start an orphanage for homeless children."

"But wealthy blokes can *afford* that generosity," Freemantle, sneering, quickly countered. "For poor men such as myself and others who are standing around here at this very moment, it means sacrifice, it means taking food from our loved ones."

"And that is a wonderful gift when you give it, for the reasons you mention," Henry assured him. "But do not presume to prevent a wealthy man from indulging the better side of his nature and—"

"Do their kind even have a better side, as you call it?" Freemantle interrupted.

Henry paused, looking disdainfully at the other man.

"Perhaps the rich would give more often if the poor did not talk so harshly about them behind their backs."

Freemantle's face was reddening, but he stepped aside as Selwyn's servants approached and started to help Cyril and Henry up a nearby slope to the awaiting carriage. In a matter of minutes, the two of them were inside a formidable castle that was a few square feet smaller than Cyril's own. Though he was finally safe, he was not so much thinking of the good food that would soon be placed before him, or the medicine that would treat the scratches, cuts, and bruises over much of his body, or the rest in a clean bed that undoubtedly would come soon. Rather, his mind was in two other places almost at the same time: home with his wife and daughters at his side, but, yes, also, that beach near the white cliffs of Dover, and the two whales dying on it.

CHAPTER 4

They decided, initially, that nothing could be done to help the whales. Because of their size and great weight, there seemed to be no way of getting them back into the water. Henry, in particular, was distressed by this but he, too, realized that it was one of those great tragedies that happens in nature. This occurrence added a special poignancy, but the result was the same: the death of two creatures who were part of the family of largest mammals in the world. . .

Lord Nigel Selwyn had finished using a thin sliver of sanded wood to pick his teeth after having peppered his guests with questions about their journey and the shipwreck itself.

"I am completely alone, isolated," he told his two unexpected visitors a short while after they had joined him at the dinner table, a table that was every bit as large as found in the homes of other lords of that day, a table where he generally would sit by himself, waited on by his full staff of servants.

He looked with great wistfulness about the dining hall, seeing the relative emptiness whereas, elsewhere, one of that elegance, with its thick walls of imported wood, its cathedral ceiling, with a skylight of stained glass in the center, might have been crammed from wall-to-wall with people, multiple conversations, the odors of food.

"For a man to be pampered as I have been seems a blessing to be coveted," he continued. "Look at this room. Our own prime minister lives as well, or better. But how many others do? I wine and dine in the midst of luxury, yet others grovel for scraps in the dirt of London alleys."

The three of them had just devoured a meal that ranked with the best the two visitors had ever eaten: sweet and sour spiced rabbit, a second choice of roast chicken crowned with eggs, cabbage chowder, braised turnips with barley bread, rose pudding, and golden steamed custard.

After dinner, they sucked pleasantly on square pieces of pine nut candy.

"I used to covet friendships," Selwyn continued forlornly, "but I did so with an intensity that scared everyone away after a short while. My money was little more than a bribe, but no one would succumb for very long. Always they would turn their backs on me."

"You have security here that most of your countrymen do not," Cyril observed, admiring a castle that was splendidly furnished. "Is that not worth a great deal? Does that not give you some degree of peace of mind?" Cyril found himself still getting used to a man who seemed to have been thrust from medieval England into a technological age by some sort of time warp.

"Oh, it does," Selwyn agreed. "Given all that I have, I shall hardly be someone who starves to death. Nor will I ever know what it is like to exist on a pittance, thus making it unlikely that I will ever be found in some London alley."

He closed his eyes, his mood darkening.

"Instead, I wager, when they come upon my lifeless form, I will be in my own bed, dead by my own hand because I had no life beyond the walls of this castle."

He waved his hand about the dining hall.

"And what living is there for me even *inside?* I have a set daily routine, and I follow it without exception. Is that what any of the three of us could call life? A dull perpetuation, meaningless at its core?"

"So many people are walking the streets, the roads, the roving homeless in rags, their stomachs crying out," Cyril said. "Are you not blessed beyond anything those poor, lonely folk could dream of?"

"Let me tell you about that: I passed by a poor family on the way to London the other day, and I studied them until they were out of sight behind my driver and me."

"And what did you discover?"

"They were laughing. Smiles lit up their faces, dirty faces, yes, bony cheeks and all the rest. But they had managed to be happy."

Cyril felt some sympathy for the man.

"This location *is* a bit far out," he observed. "Should you not be closer to London, for example?"

"If I were a social sort of individual, Cyril, I might well find it impossible to live where I do."

Cyril had a blank expression on his face.

"Do you not know of me, Lord Fothergill?" Selwyn asked.

"I have heard little."

"And that is how I have planned it."

Selwyn did not act in a way that seemed at all content but resigned instead.

"To be set off from others as you are now?" Cyril pressed. "Are you trying to say that that is truly by choice?"

"Sometimes our choices, free as they may seem, make a prisoner of each man."

"Well said. But then you cannot deny that men have been known to be gobbled up by utter madness in prison, particularly those punished by being put in solitary confinement where they hear no voices, no sounds at all but when some so-called food is thrown at them or when rats are scurrying around the hard stone floor."

Cyril leaned forward.

"We have heard you talk over the past hour, Nigel. We have heard the words of a man whose self-imposed confinement has taken its toll on him. No man can exist entirely by himself. God made us to *need* others."

"But I have failed Him miserably," Selwyn said. "The fact remains that I am where I am, my dear fellow, and have been here for many, many years. I am fifty-two now, and have had no one at my side except hired help for more than half that time. My parents died of some disease for which doctors still have no name."

Selwyn stood and, after stretching his legs to rid them temporarily of pain in the knees, slowly walked around the table to the sole single-paned window in that small dining hall, a beautiful work of art imported from Venice, clear glass with beveled edges bordered by pieces of glass of varying sizes, shapes, and hues.

"I stand here each night and look out over the channel and see some vessels passing by out there on the ageless water," he said, "some folk walking the beach, an occasional family of whales in the middle of a kind of ballet in the moonlight. Have you ever seen those creatures perform so wondrously, Lord Fothergill?"

Smiling knowingly, Cyril nodded in Henry's direction, who asked humbly, "May I respond to that, Lord Selwyn?"

"Of course. I am not king or prime minister or archbishop. You need not secure permission from me. I shall sit down and listen fully to what you want to say."

Henry proceeded to tell of the singular experiences that Cyril and he had had with the mother whale and baby. The other man was fascinated and seemed disappointed when Henry had come to the end of the tale.

"I am aware of certain individuals who are at the indefensible point of near-worship concerning whales," Selwyn commented. "But do not include me in this blasphemy! They may be grand creations from the mind of the Creator Himself, but they are hardly the stuff of gods. I would never be a party to such heathenism!"

He paused, choosing his words with care. "Nevertheless, I do find whales most intriguing, gentlemen."

"In what way?" Cyril inquired.

"They go on their way, in their own strange and endless world, and if it were not for human beings and a few aggressive sharks from time to time, they would have no real enemies, and they certainly would not bother anyone."

Nigel was transparently jealous of the whales' apparent freedom. Nothing bound these creatures except the ties that seemed to exist between them. If they became tired of one place, they could move on to another, and since they dominated every body of water they entered, they had no scarcity of food.

He turned to Cyril.

"They *are* dying out there on the beach, you know. It may take hours, it may be as much as a day, but they *will* die."

He hesitated, obviously emotionally stirred by their plight.

"Unless we can somehow get them back into the Channel," Nigel said after a few seconds.

Cyril was greatly moved but recognized the problems that any would-be rescuers were certain to face.

"Mere men could not move creatures of their bulk," he mused, his heart beating faster at the notion. "And these are not babies to be flung about by their watchful mothers."

Selwyn considered this while pondering an alternative.

"Wait, my brothers! Think of this, if you will: I own a large fleet of ships," he told them excitedly. "Nearly half the fleet are anchored right now at the harbor only a few miles south of here. I can bring any number here that I want."

"Flat-bottom boats are best in shallow water," Henry remarked almost casually. "They could get in pretty close."

"I have a number of those!" Selwyn exclaimed.

"With long enough ropes, I imagine, to wrap around their large bodies—" Cyril was racing ahead to what could be done.

"In that event, we just might be able to drag both of those whales back to where the water of the channel is deeper, and they could swim away if they have not been damaged too severely by what has happened," Henry said.

The two other men looked at him and Henry reacted sheepishly, not quite sure what had transpired then.

"Did I say something wrong?" he asked defensively.

"You said something very right," Cyril assured him. "A wonderful idea, Lord Selwyn!"

"Thank you, Lord Fothergill. But do call me Nigel. Besides, Henry here seems to have had the idea at about the same time as I did. Your friend deserves some credit as well."

"He does indeed. As for calling you Nigel, I could certainly agree but only if you would call me Cyril in turn."

Pleased by this, Selwyn nodded with some energy, a cheerful expression supplanting what had been mostly a somber one throughout the meal.

"I shall, Cyril, I shall," he replied. "Let me send my messenger immediately. It will take through the night and into the morning for all this to be put together, but at least there is some hope. I want three of my most veteran captains back here with the appropriate vessels as soon as possible, and no excuses from either of them!"

Against all expectations, Cyril slept well for the first time in a number of weeks. And he would have done so for a longer period if he had not awakened in a sweat just before noon.

"Elizabeth!" he said, sitting up and almost shouting his wife's name. "Elizabeth, were you calling for me—?"

Then he fell back in bed.

I have to get back to you, he thought. *I cannot allow myself to linger here any longer.*

Cyril was about to sit up again when a sound touched his ears, a sad, desperate sound.

The whales!

He recognized it instantly, jumped out of bed, and slipped on some clothes that Selwyn had made available, though the shirt and pants were tight, and he was glad that he would be home soon to wear those that had been tailored for him. As he was heading into the hallway outside his room, he found Henry hurrying toward him.

"What is wrong with them?" he asked. "Can you tell?"

"They seem to be in great pain," Cyril responded. "They must have sustained injuries that we know nothing about—"

The sound was louder now, a moaning undercurrent to it.

Selwyn was outside already, watching in disbelief from the terrace of his castle.

"Those bloody awful barbarians!" he said as he heard the two men behind him.

Cyril was about to ask what was wrong when he noticed for himself. Several of the poor men of that area, including

Derek Freemantle, were starting to carve up the whales.

Abruptly, Henry turned away, physically ill. Selwyn reached out, after the heaving had stopped, and put his arm around the other man's shoulder.

"Do not be ashamed," he said with a tenderness that seemed unusual.

Only Cyril was not sick, though he was no less devastated as anger got control of him, blind, raging anger.

"Would you get your guards to—?" he started to say.

"They are on the way, Cyril," Selwyn told him. "Look!"

Half a dozen fully suited knights were riding onto the beach.

"Bless you. . ." Cyril said.

Selwyn nodded in acknowledgment.

Cyril started down the pathway from the castle, Henry just behind him.

Watching them, Selwyn hesitated, every instinct telling him that others could handle the matter, that there was no reason for him to get his hands dirty.

"My instincts have been wrong most of the years of my monkish life!" he declared out loud. "It has to stop! It has to stop or I will do the deed I have thought more and more, ending this miserable life of mine. No longer will I be a slave to the voices in my head seeking to destroy me when my heart should rule instead."

After hastening inside the castle, he grabbed a curved Saracen sword with a ruby and emerald encrusted handle and headed back outside, demanding a horse from one of his stablemen who then scurried to obey.

The two whales were surrounded by men hacking away at them. The animals were helpless before the onslaught of knives, cleavers, and hatchets.

"*Stop!*" the lead pseudo-knight demanded. "Lord Selwyn demands that you stop this—"

Derek Freemantle swung around, a long, thick-bladed knife in one hand, a slab of dripping whale meat in the other.

"I know you, Erik Lofton!" he said. "You aren't a wealthy man. You take crumbs from the table of your little master and act as though he has somehow greatly blessed you. How ignorant can you be, man?"

The knight dismounted and approached Freemantle.

"I have known no other life than this for decades, and I have no guilt over what I have chosen for myself, nor feel I shame because I am comfortable with it," he said. "I have seen wealthy men and I have seen those who are poor. Men can be noble or men can be human swine, whether rich or poor. You call the man I serve my little master. If he be that, then what shall I call you, for you are smaller still?"

Freemantle raised his knife. Immediately the other knights grabbed hold of their lances, prepared to throw them at a single command.

"You would wound me and the others here because of these brute beasts?" Freemantle said disbelievingly. "We live in hard times. We are a bunch of homeless people, and we need food anywhere, anyway we can get it. We kill cattle, horses, whatever we can get our hands on. Are we not more important than brute beasts?"

"I would bind you up and haul you off to jail if my lord demanded it of me!" the knight declared in such a way as to dispel any doubt.

At that moment Cyril arrived and he spoke up.

"They saved our *lives!*" he rebuked the man. "What reward is this?"

"The reward is *ours!*" Freemantle shouted. "These beasts will provide needed oil for our lamps and food for the stomachs of the families of every man standing here. Your lives were saved, and now ours will be for a time."

"At what price?" Cyril demanded.

Everyone was stunned into silence by what had suddenly started to happen with the slightly smaller of the two whales.

She was moaning horribly, fluids of various colors oozing from the gashes in her side, whole chunks of flesh torn from her before the ravaging could be stopped. Despite this, she was trying to move, obviously in agony, but not stopping.

"What is going on?" Selwyn said, now standing between Cyril and Henry.

"I have no idea," Cyril answered, "death spasms or—"

Henry stepped forward.

"Birth. . ." he said, shaking his head sadly. "This one is trying to give birth to her baby before she dies."

"How could you know anything like *that?*" Freemantle asked, unnerved. "How—?"

Henry tapped his forehead.

"I feel this one's pain," he said.

Freemantle snorted at that.

"You are as dumb as these foul beasts of the sea," he remarked with a disdain that he did nothing to hide but trotted it out like some kind of weapon. "That you look and act like a human being is an insult to the rest of us!"

Henry reached out and grabbed the other man's wrist, tightening his long, bony fingers around it.

"Should we have *rejected* their help because they were not like you and the other butchers you have brought with you?" he challenged. "Right now I think you and the other bloodthirsty louts are the ones who appear to be less than human."

"Let go of me!" Freemantle demanded.

Freemantle was taken away but most of his supporters chose to remain. The confrontation between Henry and Freemantle had made their mood uglier than before. They joined ranks and formed a circle around the two whales.

"Will you kill us along with our families by denying them the food they need?" one of the men called out.

Another added scornfully, "You seem more concerned about those creatures out in the channel than men, women, and poor little children right here on land. These are times of hunger. Crops are failing. There is even talk of disease!"

At that, Cyril's throat muscles tightened. He could not help but wonder if anything had been leaked accidentally by someone within the Houses of Parliament or from No.

10 Downing Street in some deliberate manner by those who were behind the plague plot in the first place.

"It cannot be right, you people threatening us like this with your presence, trying to stop us the way you are," the unidentified man continued. "You, with your lackey knights, coming here from your fancy castle up there on the white cliffs to deny us what these whales can provide! Surely you all run the risk of Almighty God's judgment!"

Cyril had had enough.

"It is not the food you seek that enrages me," he said, "but the ruthless way you are getting it. It is not that you care little for the pain of these creatures but that you care not at all. And now one of you tries to frighten everyone by hinting at some kind of disease."

That same man walked to within a yard of Cyril. He had a long face, with a beard that made him look like a figure from the Old Testament. His shoulders were narrow, and he had a voice that seemed to have to struggle to be heard, which meant that he tended to talk in a perpetually strident manner.

"If the truth frightens, then should we suppress it for what some consider the greater good?" he stated. "I am called Angus Hooten, and I have been a Christian for many years, sir. I strive to follow the example of Jesus Christ who was Truth in the flesh. Anything else is deception, and I have chosen not to deceive anyone."

Nerve ends tingled on the back of Cyril's neck. The man's manner was impressive but there was in it the hint of rote.

"But what makes you believe that 'talk' such as you have mentioned should be made legitimate by a public airing if it is nothing more than heresy or idle gossip?" he countered, realizing how he had come across information that had started him on this extraordinary odyssey. Cyril wanted to find out whether this man was all bluff or really did have "ways" of getting information, the sources of which were faintly ominous.

"I have my sources," the other man insisted.

"Then enlighten us."

"I overheard some men talking."

Cyril laughed loudly but only for the benefit of the people around him.

"That is not enough to justify trying to—" he started to say.

The sudden birth of a baby whale interrupted him.

The little whale was partially out of its womb when the mother shuddered once, twice, a third time, and though she did not die just then, she had no strength left to help her little one.

"He will suffocate if we just stand here," Cyril said as he started to push Angus Hooten to one side.

But Hooten was a strong man, a scrappy fighter, having proven himself in many a pub brawl despite his protestations of Christian faith, and it was easy for him to land a fist in Cyril's stomach before two of the knights were able to get down from their horses and restrain him.

As this was going on, no one seemed to notice Henry quietly making his way to the rear of the mother whale. Sitting down in the sand, with salt water lapping over his legs, he grabbed hold of the infant's tail and started pulling.

"I need help!" he exclaimed. "Will someone not help me?"

Everyone stood where they were, transfixed by the sight: Henry, with tears cascading down his cheeks, was trying to pull the baby out the rest of the way.

Throwing an elaborate knit cape which had covered his shoulders to one of the nearby knights, Nigel Selwyn abruptly strode forward and sat down next to Henry.

"Show me what to do!" he declared with unaccustomed enthusiasm. "I have never birthed a whale before!"

People laughed, poor men and women, veteran knights joining together. Only Angus Hooten balked, a look of disdain marring his features.

"Just grab the back end about six inches above my hands," Henry told him, "and pull as I am doing, pull with all you have. . .sir."

"After all these years," Selwyn remarked, "I shan't say how much I do have left in me, young man, but this little creature *will* have it all."

And so the two men struggled, as the baby whale struggled, the mother unable to help any longer. She could only look and wonder, and wait for death.

"Cut the beast. . ." a female voice called out.

At first neither Henry nor Selwyn knew what that meant.

"The birth opening," the same voice added. "I know what it is called in a woman but not a whale, for heaven's sake."

An ample-figured woman pushed through the crowd.

"Give it more room," she told them.

"We have no knives," Henry told her.

"A sword will do," she said. Turning around, she asked of the knights, "What brave soul among you will give me his sword or dagger?"

Before a second had passed, she was holding a large dagger, which each knight carried as a secondary weapon, and had bent down next to mother and child.

"I have performed Caesareans on many a woman," she announced, "but I need your prayers for *this* one."

The knights climbed down from their steeds and knelt just shy of the mudlike sand. Most of the gathered poor, some reluctantly, did likewise, directly behind them. Only Angus Hooten expressed his contempt by turning his back and leaving the beach. The woman cut away determinedly at the whale's thick hide and did so with an expertise that surprised even her. In little more than a minute and a half the baby whale had popped completely out from its mother and was lying on the sand, wiggling like an oversized guppy at first. Then it stopped moving altogether.

"We have to get this little one out to sea without delay," Henry observed.

"But it surely will sink and drown this soon after birth," Cyril told him. "From what I have heard, baby whales swim soon enough but only by the side of their mother, not completely alone as it shall be with strange creatures such as us all around it."

"It will not drown!"

"You must come to your senses. You—"

Henry glowered at his friend for assuming that he was not in full command of what he was saying.

"*They* will help!" he announced defiantly and with some pride as he pointed farther out in the channel.

Six fins outlined against the clear morning sky!

"Look!" someone gasped out loud.

Everyone turned their attention in that same direction.

"Now do you see what I mean?" Henry pronounced triumphantly.

A chorus of sounds started, sounds both familiar and strange to Cyril and Henry, from the group of whales that seemed to be waiting some distance offshore.

Aghast, Cyril looked at them as though they were figments of his imagination. He blinked several times but the fins did not vanish.

What is it, Lord, that binds these creatures together? he prayed. *And what does man do to them in the meantime? Kill them, use their fluids to fuel his lamps, their very flesh itself for food. Is that why You put them into the seas and oceans of this world? Is their ultimate purpose to serve the human race in some manner, shape, or form?*

"Help us!" Henry said.

Finally recovered from the blow to his stomach, Cyril hurried over to them.

"What do I do?" he asked.

"Get your arms *under* the front," Henry instructed, "while we do the same with the rear."

Henry waited a few moments then called out, "Lift! Now!"

The three of them got the little whale barely up off the sand but struggled to take it out to where the water was deep enough that it could float on its own.

Someone else joined them, not able to wait any longer . . .the knight named Erik Lofton.

Finally they were able to move the baby a few feet, but the water at that point was still not deep enough for it to have any hope of swimming on its way.

"Look at that!" one of the women shouted, breaking the momentary silence.

"*They are moving!*" an astonished-sounding male voice yelled at full volume.

The four men holding the baby whale could not risk stopping to get a good look at what was happening with the awaiting whales. It was wise for them only to continue walking, inch by inch, under the substantial weight of the baby whale.

But that did not keep Henry from speaking up.

"Trying to get closer. . ." he said, "trying to help us."

"But that would be impossible," Nigel Selwyn reminded him. "The water is too shallow right here. They, too, will be stranded if they do not stop."

"It does not matter," added Henry. "They know only one thing right now, and care about little else. What they hear are the dying cries of two of their own kind, and the frightened squeals of another just come into this world."

Almost on cue, the whales resumed their plaintive cries. And the baby responded, as life seemed once again to flow through its body. Only its mother was silent, her brain overwhelmed by the pain that assaulted her from every part of her body.

Looking conspiratorial, Selwyn whispered something into Lofton's ear and the knight left immediately.

"Where is *he* going?" Cyril asked, frowning. "What in the world could you have told that man?"

"You will find out soon enough," Selwyn replied with an exaggerated imperiousness.

Lofton sent another knight to take his place with the baby whale, then ordered two of those remaining to stand on each side of the mother, and two others to stand next to the second adult whale. Each knight had a crossbow attached to his saddle.

Suddenly Cyril comprehended what Selwyn was planning.

He was getting ready to protest when he realized that, however cold the other man's efficiency seemed, it *was* the only way, and had to be done quickly or else the intruding whales would keep swimming toward shore, and become victims as the previous ones had been.

Selwyn gave the order and each of the four knights shot an arrow in his crossbow through the eyes of each whale, as Maximilian Letchworth had done with a whale pole a week before. The huge mammals lifted themselves off the sand, in their last shuddering gasps of pain, before falling back, the larger whale dead immediately.

The mother lingered for a few seconds allowing her to look toward the channel, as she tried to see what was happening to her child, before she rested her head with a curious gentleness on the wet sand, and was finally free of pain.

Even those poor men and women who had been antagonistic previously were so moved that their sobs filled the air. And that included Angus Hooten, who dropped to his knees.

The knights responsible for delivering the fatal shots allowed their crossbows to slip from their hands and turned away, trying to restrain their emotions in front of the crowd.

Nigel Selwyn returned to the water, resuming his position at the side of the baby whale.

"You need not do this," he told Erik Lofton.

"I would be pleased to stay, Lord Selwyn."

"If that is what you would like to do."

"It is what I feel I *must* do, sir."

Without warning, the six whales which had been heading toward the beach stopped and hesitated briefly as though communicating among themselves. The group then headed straight toward the four men who were struggling to hold onto the baby while carrying it as far offshore as they could.

One of the adult whales circled them.

"It is trying to determine what we are doing," Henry told the others.

"Absurd!" Cyril replied. "How could that be? And how could you know if it were?"

"St. Francis had no barriers between him and other living creatures."

"That may be, my brother, but this is hardly like anything *he* could have known."

The whale continued around them, making a complete circle three times.

"We cannot hold the baby much longer," Cyril protested.

And then that one whale came within a yard of Henry, the top of its head out of the water.

"Studying us," Henry remarked.

"You perhaps," Cyril said. "I think it ignores the rest of us."

Then the whale rejoined the others, the six of them forming a circle around the four men and their burden. Those on shore gawked at a sight that none would ever see repeated.

"Are they going to attack?" Cyril spoke for everyone, feeling awkward, though, for voicing a concern when the sea creatures had shown themselves only to be benevolent during past encounters with them.

Henry's face froze.

"What is it?" Cyril asked, wondering if the other man had somehow changed his mind about the whales' purpose.

"They intend to defend this baby," Henry guessed tensely but with an intuitive ability that Cyril had learned at last never to dismiss out of hand. "But by doing that, the rest of us at the same time."

"Defend us? From what?"

Erik Lofton answered instead.

"There!" he said. "To the left. *Look!*"

Another group of fins, but not those of protective whales, were visible.

"Are we ever to be rid of them?" Cyril reacted with an understandable weariness.

"Sooner, I suspect, than you will see the last of this Gervasio character," Henry told him. "If we survive, that is."

Trying not to think of their vulnerability—out in the water, no weapons to use, carrying a baby that must weigh at least 500 pounds—Cyril added, "How glad I will be when I stand overlooking hundreds of acres of dry solid land, and glimpse not so much as a fish pond nearby! Gervasio can send whatever he wants against me then. I shall be prepared, for he will have to face me on *my* turf!"

In a short while the attack began. . . .

CHAPTER 5

The sharks they saw initially were only the first of the number summoned to that location by whatever special link bound these creatures in a common hunger.

"What could be drawing them?" Cyril puzzled in vain. "There has been no blood shed here or anywhere else nearby."

But Henry had another idea.

"I am afraid that you have forgotten the fluids from the two whales on the beach," he reminded the other man.

"But there has hardly been enough time for—"

"It does not take long," Henry interrupted. "My brother demonstrated that one afternoon a few years ago, and I shall never forget that moment. Maximilian gave himself a small cut on the arm, soaked a piece of cotton fabric with blood, tied a piece of rope to this, and dangled it just above the water line."

Cyril was frowning.

"How long before the sharks came?" he asked.

"Not longer than ten minutes could have passed," Nigel Selwyn spoke up. "Having heard what you just said, I am very much afraid that I may be at fault in this predicament."

He held up his hand. There was a slight cut in the area of the thumb, with a thin trickle of blood coming from it.

"I have no idea how this happened," he told the others. "But as you can see, I have been adding the tiniest drops of blood to this water ever since I waded back in."

The sharks kept coming, as many as fifteen of them ready for the battle.

"We should retreat back to shore," Henry observed. "Sharks can do very well in shallow water since their bodies are long and trim, not bloated like the whales, but we want to make it as difficult as possible for them. Even they must stop at some point, or be beached."

The baby whale appeared apparently strengthened by being back in the channel again, where its body could absorb oxygen from the water, but it could not pull free of the four men surrounding it.

"If the sharks do attack," Selwyn added, "we can survive only if these whales actually do what they seem ready to do. Otherwise, for the sake of our own survival, we shall have to leave this poor baby and head back to shore as soon as possible."

Shouting. . . .people were shouting but not from behind them.

"I forgot about my messenger!" Selwyn yelled. "He reached my captains. Now look at those vessels. . .are they not the most beautiful sight in the world?"

Ahead. Boats. The flatbedded boats that Nigel Selwyn had demanded from his fleet. Three of these.

"Sometimes putting the fear of God into those who work for you is not such a bad thing!" Selwyn exclaimed.

The sharks were now sandwiched between the whales and the boats but seemed oblivious, bent only on what time had taught them extraordinarily well: getting more food into their bellies, whatever the risks, and then moving on to the next kill and the one after that.

"My captains have encountered those devils before," Selwyn commented, his eyes widening with sudden pride. "Be assured that they know what to do."

Captains and crews alike were well-rehearsed accordingly, but not in the necessity of dealing with whales at the same time, except to have to defend themselves against the rare ones that, for reasons unknown, attacked their boats.

As far as they were concerned, there was no difference between the threat posed by the sharks and that of the whales!

And so the men onboard the three vessels treated both species alike, ignorant of any alternative. . .by killing as many as they could aim at accurately with their harpoonlike poles.

To his horror, Selwyn then saw what was happening.

"For the love of God, no, you fools, no!" he screamed as

loudly as he could, but he was not heard by anyone.

Two sharks had already been killed and one whale had been hit. Its mighty body rose out of the water, dumbly trying to shake the metal-edged pole out of its eye socket.

"This will not continue!" Selwyn shouted. "*This will not!*"

He noticed a temporarily open section of water, with neither shark nor whale in his way, and started to swim through it.

Cyril tried to stop him.

"Nigel, no, the sharks are maddened. They could turn in that direction any minute."

"I have run nameless gauntlets before," Selwyn told him. "This one is little different from all the others."

Cyril persisted, but the other man paid no attention and after a few seconds he was too far away to hear Cyril at all.

In the blind confusion of what was happening, sharks took to attacking their wounded fellow sharks. The water was being churned to a foam that sparkled with a variety of colors under the morning sun, pieces of jagged scraps of flesh floating on the surface.

Selwyn did not allow himself to look to one side or the other, his attention locking on one of the three boats less than a hundred feet directly ahead.

Yea, though I walk through the valley of the shadow of death, I shall fear no evil, for Thou art with me, he repeated to himself. *Now, Lord, more than ever!*

A second whale was hit and leaped in agony, then hit the water barely three feet away from the "path" that Selwyn had taken, the force of its impact tossing him into the air to land nearly as close to one of the sharks.

One of the crew members on the ship toward which he had been heading saw him.

"*God in heaven!*" the man said. "*Lord Selwyn is out there now and he is—!*"

Another crew member lost no time and swung a pole in the direction of that shark, throwing the weapon swiftly. The metal edge, jagged and deadly, struck its target just as the creature was starting to close its jaws around Selwyn's right leg. Hanging on for an instant, the shark, nearly dead, let go and swam blindly toward the slaughterhouse that the rest of the channel in that immediate area had become.

"Hold on, sir, hold on!"

Someone else was shouting that from the ship an instant before he jumped overboard and swam toward the wounded lord.

Selwyn barely heard him.

"My leg!" he cried out. "My leg. . .I can feel nothing! My—!"

The man who reached him was the ship's captain.

"Sinnott!" Selwyn said. "Get back onboard. You shall not sacrifice yourself for the likes of me."

"I would die for you any other time," the man replied. "Why not now, my lord?"

"I cannot—"

Selwyn tried to resist, forcing the captain to strike his jaw, stunning but not knocking him out. Then Sinnott wrapped his left arm around Selwyn's waist and dragged the older man toward the ship where crew members were waiting to help them both get back onboard.

"Stop killing the whales!" Selwyn was muttering. "Stop—"

"He is confused," the captain whispered reluctantly to the crew. "He could not know what he is commanding us to do."

Finding strength that he should never have had, Selwyn pushed himself away from Sinnott.

"Calm down, sir!" someone said with genuine alarm. "You are becoming delirious, and you risk hurting yourself even more. You must remain—"

A moment before he started coughing up blood, Selwyn managed to say, "The sharks, yes, but not the whales. Save them, they must not be destroyed!"

"Lord Selwyn, be calm, sir," the captain begged him.

"The men you see are trying to save a baby whale. You must listen to me!"

Blood gushed up past his lips.

"Do this now!" he demanded, his voice weakening. "Those whales are not enemies. They are helping, the whales *are*—"

Groaning, he fell back against the deck but reached up feebly, his hand shaking as he barely managed to grab the captain's shirt.

"Know this, Captain Sinnott," he said, "know that however close death is to me this very moment, I have not lost my mind."

"I think you have, milord, and you do not know it," Sinnott told him reluctantly. "I have lost crew members to those monsters in times past. I do not intend to do so ever again."

"But they are no threat to us!" Selwyn begged him. "You must realize that!"

But the captain was ignoring him.

"All of them!" he demanded. "*Every last bloody one!*"

As he spoke, he was glancing at Selwyn with a mixture of contempt and pity.

Then Sinnott directed two others, those who tended to wounds and injuries while the ship was at sea, to take Lord Selwyn to the captain's quarters and treat him as well as the circumstances allowed until they could get him to a proper hospital which was more than an hour away.

They were adept as temporary nurses, having gained experience by patching up an assortment of wounds during the years of their service, these two roughneck men of the sea, often in the middle of the ocean, with physicians days or weeks away.

They quickly spread a long-favored antiseptic made of specially prepared tree sap on the wound which, though it caused the loss of a great deal of blood, was not so bad that it threatened to cause the loss of Lord Selwyn's leg.

"He will have an ugly scar," one of them observed.

"Better that than no leg at all," the other reminded.

While they were talking, medicating his wound and then bandaging it, Nigel Selwyn struggled against the unconsciousness that seemed to grab him, then let go, then grab him again and—

"I have to stop this somehow," his mind shouted. *"Oh, Lord, help me stop what they are going to do to those poor creatures."*

Even from a distance, Cyril could guess what was happening and he was convinced that little could be done. But Henry had other ideas. Without alerting anyone, he swam away from the baby whale and toward the carnage, turning briefly to call back, "Pray for me. . .as never before!"

It did not take Henry long, despite his tired condition, to reach the two remaining whales, approaching them from behind, one to his left, the other his right. They seemed to accept him on the spot—by paying no attention to him at all.

"You down there," Captain Sinnott yelled. "You are in danger! Get away, you bloody fool!"

"From you, yes, but not these creatures," Henry replied.

"You mock me, stranger," he replied. "You should know that men mock me only at their own risk."

"There is no risk to mocking someone so misguided that—" Henry spat the words at him.

"Get out of here this very moment, or I may *accidentally* hit you instead of either whale," Sinnott shot back with a sneer.

His first mate whispered something into his ear, and nodding, Sinnott seemed to regret being so harsh.

"Look, whoever you are, come onboard, and let us talk some more," he said, sounding remarkably more sympathetic. "I *will* listen, have no doubt about that."

Smiling exuberantly, and trusting most men as always, Henry left the company of the whales and swam the short distance remaining to the ship. Curiously, he felt emboldened, his blood stirred by the challenge given to him.

Father God, are You trying to prove my worth to me, my courage, whatever else You think necessary, he thought, *so that I can let go of this cloud of awful worthlessness that has smothered me all my life? Maximilian did his best but he never fully succeeded.*

As Henry was being helped onto the deck, he said, a little breathlessly, "Thank you, Captain, now let me tell you what has been—"

"Take him below," Sinnott ordered coldly, without listening. "And keep him in chains until I say otherwise."

"But you told me—" Henry protested.

"I lied!" the other man replied.

Before Henry could defend himself, two muscular crewmen grabbed him and started dragging him away.

"Those whales!" someone else yelled. "It looks as though they are getting ready to ram the ship, Captain! Remember what happened near Madagascar?"

"Of course I do," Sinnott yelled. "I was the captain then, right?"

"Right, sir, right you are!"

"Take care of both whales," Sinnott ordered. "I want this nonsense done with now. And yes, go to my cabin and check on Lord Selwyn. He has lost much blood. Unless we get a physician to treat him soon, he will die!"

Although it did seem that the whales were heading toward the ship to ram it, suddenly they disappeared, only to reappear where they had started, next to Cyril and Erik Lofton.

"They are trying to spook us!" a crew member called out.

"I think you might be right," Sinnott agreed. "But I will not be *toyed* with by some brute beast!"

"You can surely call them that, brute beasts, for sure, but can you continue to call them devils?" Henry asked as he got back to his feet. "Are they not just defending themselves? That was a warning, Captain. Can you not see the truth?"

Captain Sinnott stalked over to him and, while Henry's arms were being held tight, spit in his face.

"No one with a crippled mind like yours should dare to

contradict *me!*" he said. "You might be fine in some circus where you could be a serviceable clown perhaps, but out here, among normal men, you are just a—"

"My dear brother was a captain," Henry interrupted, "but nothing like you."

"Oh, a captain, you say. And what silly fantasy is this?"

"It is the truth, you know," Henry, smiling, said.

"His name, give us his name, so that we all can hear what a liar you are in addition to being stupid."

Another voice answered for Henry.

"Letchworth. . ." it said sternly, "Maximilian Letchworth. Now, Captain Sinnott, try to convince everyone standing here that you do not know *his* name."

Sinnott swung around and faced Nigel Selwyn who had regained consciousness and managed to stumble outside, though his weak condition was obvious.

"Henry was on nearly every voyage that the fabled Captain Letchworth took," he continued. "He probably knows more about seafaring that any man here, including you, Mr. Sinnott. He is not what many men are, I admit, but in *your* case, he should be considered fortunate, because he has not been contaminated by your arrogance."

Selwyn was wavering.

"Those whales *cannot* be slaughtered like the rest," he said. "You must stop this mindless carnage, Captain Sinnott."

Each step meant pain as Lord Selwyn approached Sinnott.

"As your captain—" the other man started to say.

"To which I respond," Selwyn interrupted, "as some unlearned souls might say simply, Sinnott, you ain't my captain no more. I want you to step aside *now!* Any delay will result in disgrace that I personally shall mete out."

But Sinnott refused to listen.

"You have been made mad by pain," he said. "You are not in control of yourself. Therefore, I choose to ignore your rantings."

He pointed to two other crew members.

"Take him back to my cabin and this time make sure that

he stays there. Lord Selwyn must not be allowed to harm himself. We are his protectors now, and any man on this ship who fails in that regard will be punished."

The blow that Selwyn delivered to Sinnott's jaw was hardly a knockout punch, since this would have been impossible for someone in his condition, but it had sufficient power to spin the captain to one side though he remained standing.

Selwyn lurched toward the railing.

"I think now that there is only one course of action I can take that will *compel* you all to believe me," he said, his voice loud, and without a trace of trembling.

Everyone onboard froze where they stood, including Sinnott, not one believing that a man like Nigel Selwyn would be capable of such an act.

Then he started to lift himself up over the railing. No one knew whether Selwyn was bluffing. But that scarcely mattered. Considering what had happened to him, and a fragile physical condition that could turn fatal at any time, it was remarkable that he was doing anything but resting in the captain's cabin until he could be treated by physicians on land.

"Good-bye. . ." he started to say. "My fate is in the hands of the One who—"

"Stop!" Sinnott yelled at him finally.

"I must follow my heart," Selwyn said. "There have been too many times when I thought it was enough just to keep going from day to day, little more than existing perhaps, but not enough to make me glad that I was able to get up each morning.

"Until now, I preferred not to awaken at all most of the time, but rather, to be found quite dead by my butler or my maid or one of the other two dozen people I have been trying to pretend cared anything at all about me. I have two dining halls that can entertain a hundred people, but no one ever joins me for a repast. I eat alone, I sleep alone, there are no children who bear my name.

"You all earn good wages because of me, but none of you has any idea who I really am, as a man, perhaps because I have not been sure myself. And I know nothing about anyone here. I am just that strange chap who hides himself away like a hermit in his cliff-top castle. I live, I die, it is of no concern to any of you."

He pointed to the whales which remained near Cyril and Erik Lofton who were by then struggling to keep the baby from sinking.

"They seem somehow more human than I," Selwyn went on, "though they are little more than sea creatures, mere animals. How much have *I* ever sacrificed for another soul? But look at what they have given up today!"

His condition was worsening.

"I shall go now, to my death or whatever else it is that our God has decreed," he said, "but I make that decision out of a caring heart, a heart that embraces those whales far more than I have wanted to embrace any human being."

As Selwyn began to tumble over the edge, strong hands grabbed him under the shoulders and started to pull him up, and he was far too weak to protest any rescue.

He fell into Sinnott's arms as soon as he was back on deck.

"I feel so ashamed," he sobbed. "How can you have any respect for me now that you know the kind of fool I have been all these years, and this from my own lips? Death so near makes reason take flight."

Sinnott's manner had changed wholly, his own eyes starting to fill up with tears.

"Be still, my lord, be still," he said softly.

Selwyn struggled but was now barely able to lift his arms.

"How can I be still?" he asked. "You will kill those splendid beings as soon as I am locked away in your quarters and I can do nothing to make you stop. If I must *die* trying to stop you, I shall—"

"Say nothing further," the captain whispered, placing two fingers gently on the other man's thin, pale lips.

Then he added, his voice breaking, "What we have seen,

my lord, what we have heard from you now is enough to cause any man to stand back and salute you."

"Salute?" Selwyn repeated. "You must be a bit daft yourself! I would have thought you more inclined to laugh me to scorn as a result of my ramblings, and instead abandon me to the mercy of those whales below."

Sinnott turned and glanced at the men behind him.

"Tell him how you feel, mates," he said, though not as an order. "Tell Lord Selwyn so that he will understand what is on *your* hearts. Do that now, will you?"

Selwyn's eyelids were nearly closing, his vision fading, ghastly pain pummeling his brain.

Be my strength, oh, Savior, for just another moment, he begged. *Please do not deny me this, precious Lord Jesus!*

As every crew member saluted him, he reflected that might have been a good way for someone such as he to die, at last experiencing what he hungered after the greater part of his life. But death was not to take him anytime soon, for he would recover from those wounds. . .and then, in the midst of the coming holocaust, this little man called Lord Nigel Selwyn would live as never before.

CHAPTER 6

The grisly operation on his leg was performed less than forty minutes after Nigel Selwyn was taken to the only hospital near his estate.

While none of the surgeons had previously treated anyone for shark bite, one of them said, "When you get down to it, is there much difference between what has happened to Lord Selwyn and someone who has been attacked by a rabid dog? At least there is no danger of Lord Selwyn going mad."

Another danger was present. . .that he would lose his leg . . .but the surgeons had a personal interest: Lord Selwyn was a frequent benefactor to the hospital, paying for badly needed high-tech equipment and an expansion of the main building.

Cyril and Henry stayed with him before the operation.

"I am dying!" he shouted periodically. "I never wanted to die alone, especially now. . . though I thought that that was to be my destiny. . . .Someone. . .please. . .will someone take my hand. . .so that I know. . .I am not alone?"

Henry glanced at one of the surgeons who nodded, and then he gently folded his hands around Nigel's and whispered to him, "Even if we were not here right now, you still would have Someone, my brother."

Selwyn did not have the energy even to sob, for the pain was draining him of everything but his melancholy.

"Yes, yes. . .I know. . .but your hand. . .your hand. . .it does feel so good to me now. . .so warm," Selwyn said haltingly, "so kind. . .and gentle, your touch. . .and loving. . .I have never coveted the love of another man. . .because I was ashamed of needing it. . . ."

"Jonathan and David loved one another," Henry reminded him. "And remember, Christ loved the apostle John."

"I know that. . .yes, I do. . .but those were special days. . . unlike what we have now. . .we live. . .in a rankly different world . . .more sinful times besieging us. . .it is not like it once was. . . ..we have lost so much. . .we have lost—"

Then another wave of blackness claimed him as he was about to be wheeled into the operating room.

"I can feel his fear," Henry remarked moments later.

"I find it a bit more difficult," Cyril admitted.

"Because you have had people around you all your life. You have never known the cold grip of true, aching loneliness."

"That is true, Henry. And it would appear that when I die, that family of mine will be gathered around me."

Cyril did not know how any man could pass from life without familiar, loved faces surrounding him.

"To think I could go on that final journey with no one caring enough to. . .to—" he said out loud.

"People do all the time in this world," Henry reminded him.

"The wandering poor, the homeless beggars?"

"In some countries, it happens regularly. . .by the hundreds, Cyril, in a ditch by themselves, their bodies eventually cast into a pauper's grave, no tears shed, no tender touch, just like a load of manure."

"That is an *awful* thought, Henry."

"To be sure. But it is cruel reality for numberless masses of men, women, and children year after year. Being alone and unwanted makes me fear death more than I should as a Christian. And it is obvious that Nigel looks at it the same way."

"I have not thought about death to any extent, what with so much life always around me, except when I choose to be by myself for a time."

"It has been on my mind for a long time. In the past, I found myself wondering what would happen when Maximilian is gone. He was older, and it seemed likely that he would go before I did. How could I face that?"

He was stepping into self-pity but Cyril was amazed that this didn't happen more often.

"He has servants all around him," Henry continued as he

nodded toward Selwyn. "I would have no one. My home is a fraction of the size of his but it would seem far emptier."

"But it is sometimes lonelier to be in the midst of scores of hired help who do not care whether you live or die."

Henry seemed puzzled so Cyril tried to explain himself more clearly.

"I have tried to be friendly to my people, but I am quite sure that Nigel has extended no such effort, deliberately anyway. He seems scared that perhaps they will take advantage of him because they will think him 'soft.'

"So, what happens in Nigel Selwyn's life? He builds barriers, formidable ones. He ends up having many people around him but there is a barrier between him and them, something like a stone wall that he had not bothered either to scale or tear down."

Henry was shaking his head.

"What a terrible road to travel through this world," he muttered.

"Oh, I agree," Cyril told him. "This man never finds love because he never makes himself vulnerable enough that others can feel for him."

"I think that may change," Henry suggested wisely.

"I pray so. He has been in agony too long. The doctors say that he has done extraordinarily well, considering how much pain he has endured. But he has had to deal with another kind of pain all his life, and has become very good at that."

Just after the operation, as he was going in and out of consciousness again, Lord Nigel Selwyn heard someone tell him that his leg had been saved. . . .

As the two men waited for Nigel Selwyn to regain consciousness, Cyril shivered, holding himself tightly.

Millions of bodies bleeding internally, organs drowning . . .a disease that takes flight in the air, passed on currents of—

The civilized world under the grip of the Hanta virus.

Seated in a tiny room down the corridor from where Selwyn was taken after the operation, Cyril was thinking of what would happen to the entire system of socialized health care, seldom very good at its shining best, with the kind of assault likely to rise up against it. He had no doubt that it would quickly break down in a matter of weeks or months.

"If an epidemic hits, that ward will seem like a gathering of women at afternoon tea," he said dejectedly.

"But there is something else, Cyril," Henry said. "What happens if the doctors start dying by the hundreds? Who will treat the sick?"

They looked at one another.

"The Jews. . ." Cyril remarked. "They will suffer terribly."

Henry looked completely lost.

"Hatred," Cyril explained. "It has been a long time since Christ was crucified, but the Jews are still called Christ killers by more 'respectable' people than you might suspect. And such an indictment is used as an excuse for victimizing them in every way conceivable. The Holocaust was just one manifestation. Until Yeltsin, violent anti-Semitism was still being practiced, to however diminished an extent, in the Union of Soviet Socialist Republics.

"It is possible that, as with the victims of disease, there will be others who are cut down, not from germs but mindless bigotry. There is a group on the continent, which has become resurgent after virtual annihilation centuries ago. Its leaders and members profess a commitment to the annihilation of every Christian as well as every Jew. It was thought to have died out by the medieval period, but I was never convinced of this."

"Who are they, Cyril?"

"The Druids."

Henry's mouth dropped open.

"My brother suspected that they were coming back strong. Are they organized, Cyril? Or just individuals scattered around?"

"Very organized, and more dangerous than rabid dogs because they are demonically clever. I think they started surfacing during World War II. The Nazis owed a great deal to them, their anti-Semitism having its roots in the Druid cult. The link between the Druids and the Nazis was forged in occultic history, hence, the swastika or *svastikah*."

It was one of those handful of subjects that the aristocracy seldom discussed among themselves, one of those hidden "things of darkness" that nobody had the nerve to bring out in the open and deal with, not the established church, not the prime minister, not any member of Parliament, no lord or baron or anyone else. Had any Druids infiltrated the British government, secretly influencing its policies to an ever greater degree?

"I have felt the appeal of the Druids' virulent anti-Semitism myself," Cyril acknowledged, confronting a part of himself that, for a man of conscience, was profoundly disturbing.

"Despite your Christianity?" Henry asked.

"Despite that, yes. Oh, how I ache when I look the truth squarely in the face. But while bigotry is a sin, it is scarcely the only one of which our fallen natures are guilty. Consider this, though, my friend: Every time we sin—whether through bigotry or lying or promiscuity or whatever else—we prove the necessity of Christ's sacrifice. But something inside me seems to say that when the sin of which we are guilty at a given moment involves His chosen people—"

Cyril was in readily apparent anguish as he acknowledged this.

"I say to you this day, that surely it *should* be that no *Christian* is guilty of harboring such venomous feelings. But then are not Christians more likely than others because of what the *Jewish* mob demanded of Pontius Pilate? Yet I have a faith based upon forgiveness, without which God would have to deny *me* my salvation.

"I suppose, Henry, that if an entire generation in a family is anti-Semitic, then it becomes more likely, if not certain, that the one succeeding it will be as well, and the one after that, the sins of the parents being visited upon the children. Somewhere along the way, whatever specious justification might have existed at the beginning becomes muddled, and then a century or two later fades out altogether, yet the prejudice remains, foul and poisonous."

"And look at what happens in the meantime!" Henry offered.

"Human hearts have been left conditioned to look at every last Jew with loathing. It continues to this day," Cyril said, not proudly.

He felt pleased at the way Henry had been able to express himself in recent days, ever so much more eloquently than at first, and he could only assume that part of the man's problem had been that people in the past treated him as "different." They may have assumed he was mentally deficient because of some awkwardness early on, some impediment to his speech perhaps, and treated him accordingly, which did not necessarily mean in an unkind fashion. And yet Henry had been showing powers of reasoning that were virtually the equal of a well-educated person.

I wonder if anything has ever been "wrong" with him as such? Cyril thought. *Or could it just be that he failed to live up to the expectations that people had for him since he was a young child? Any boy's natural abilities can be affected positively or negatively by his environment.*

Cyril came to the realization that Henry Letchworth needed plenty of encouragement in order to blossom even more fully.

"Why, I know many poor people who go so far as to claim that they have never met a poor Jew, a homeless Jew, an orphaned Jew. And, therefore, they reason that Jews in positions of power soak up so much money that they can cause a financial panic throughout the known world anytime they want."

"I think I understand. You feel, in any gradual breakdown because of epidemics around the world, that Jews will become a target?" Henry asked.

"Yes, my brother. Scapegoats are *always* sought in times of crisis. And every Jew alive today is particularly vulnerable, should an outbreak occur. I mean, look at the strict dietary laws of Orthodox Jews, which some would say are their way of avoiding contamination, laws that would appear suspicious during any epidemic."

"Surely not!" Henry exclaimed, shocked at the sinful blindness of great masses of people.

Cyril disagreed.

"Why else would they eat kosher foods to the exclusion of any other kind?" Cyril asked. "Some would say they know what is coming, and they are savoring the possibility of getting revenge against Gentiles for all these centuries of persecution. Such is the genius of anti-Semitism, the raw, dark genius. It takes some truths, mixes in falsehoods, and dresses it all up with a few historical facts taken out of context."

More time passed. . . .

"My home is close, yet it seems half a world away," Cyril was telling Henry.

They had been trying to decide the best route to take from the southern coast of England, through to the interior, and on to home.

But they had no money.

There was no money left, they had lost everything on the ship.

And the only clothes they had left to wear were those their benefactor initially provided, their seafaring garb torn and useless.

At home, I had an entire room of clothes, Cyril thought.

Elizabeth had hers, while Clarice and Sarah shared one that was the largest of the three.

Three rooms just for the family's attire!

And this was not considered excessive since clothes were part of the statement that each lord and his family were making. Such a custom—to have the brightest clothes, the greatest variety, the most costly adornments as ribbons and leather swatches, and jewelry of every description—had continued through the centuries.

Now, though, Cyril had borrowed clothes from a

stranger. For Henry, however, those clothes were several steps up from what he normally wore.

But Cyril was far more annoyed about not having money to rent a car or buy horses to ride home. And he was not about to drop to his knees, figuratively or otherwise, before Nigel Selwyn and ask for any kind of loan.

"For nearly seventeen centuries the Fothergills have never needed anyone else's money!" he declared. "I do not intend to sully that record."

"Then I have a suggestion," Henry said.

Though fond of the other man, and impressed by his degree of intelligence, Cyril was not confident that Henry was always logical.

"Go ahead. Tell me what it is."

"I used to walk great distances," Henry remarked. "We could do it, Cyril. We could walk as far as we can manage and then sleep somewhere along the way."

"But what about food?"

"We could catch what we need."

Henry was enthusiastic.

"Rabbits, squirrels, turtles, we would have a big choice," he added, beaming.

Cyril didn't like the sound of that. He was still a member of the British aristocracy, and the notion of having to live, even for a few days, like someone who was homeless repulsed him.

"We would be beggars," he protested.

"I think otherwise, friend: We would be independent," Henry said, "owing nothing to any man."

"There has to be another way."

Nigel Selwyn provided it.

After the operation, once fully conscious and therefore coherent for more than a few minutes, he insisted upon helping them out yet again, including an offer of whatever amount of money they thought they would need.

"We are working on something else," Cyril told him evasively, "but thank you very much for offering, Nigel."

"Think of me as a hermit," Selwyn replied. "Think of me as whatever else you like, but do not insult me by supposing that I am blind or stupid."

Cyril threw up his hands in a gesture of surrender.

"Good! Erik Lofton and another of my knights will accompany you," Selwyn told them. "They are already getting my carriage, sufficient food for the trip, and a few weapons. Let me warn you that I will accept no refusal."

"But we took no weapons with us the first time around," Cyril pointed out while trying not to aggravate him.

"That was when you were able to travel with much more anonymity than will be the case this time. There can be no more secrecy. At least two dozen people now know that *something* rather strange is going on, even if most cannot fathom what in the world it might be."

He narrowed his eyes.

"And this Gervasio you mention surely has seen to it that word has been sent ahead of you."

That was something Cyril had worried about but did not share with Henry. Anyone as maniacal as the ratman was capable of whatever acts necessary to achieve his goals, and informants were ready to provide him with whatever he required.

"That may be right," he conceded. "But what about you? If you are linked with us, your life might be in danger as well."

"My remaining knights shall be more than sufficient to protect me as they will with you and Henry," Selwyn answered confidently. "If I can survive a shark attack and not be hurt by mammoth whales, I should harbor no fear about mere men. Against the shark I had no defense. And as far as the whales are concerned, I needed none."

"But we may be dealing with more than men, you know."

Selwyn's expression changed.

"I have had my manhood tested within the day," he went on, "but if you are correct, then it is what I am as a *Christian* that could next be assaulted."

Cyril and Henry were sitting on chairs beside Selwyn's bed.

It was Henry who reached out and took the other man's hand in his own.

"God will use you mightily," he said.

"But how can you be so sure?" Selwyn asked.

"Someone with a hampered mind cannot think of this?" Henry asked pointedly, bristling a bit at the implication.

"No, I did not mean that, my good man. I would have asked the same question of anyone. All of us are but pygmies in the faith compared to the original apostles. They endured far more than any of us here will face."

"But none was remarkable before Jesus took them like human clay and made them into what they became."

He leaned over the bed.

"I feel in my spirit that greatness is ahead for you," he said.

"In everything that I have done, in everything that I am, I have felt abjectly, unalterably unworthy of even the simplest contact," Selwyn admitted. "My wealth has been a shield of sorts, one without which I could not have lived as long as I have. At least, if I were lonely, I was not hungry."

Pain raced along the nerves in his leg, abused as they were by shark and surgeon alike, and his face became even more pale.

Cyril and Henry waited patiently for him to speak again.

"At least, if my emotions were raw and despairing," Selwyn went on, "I could hide myself away in the great splendor of that magnificent structure I call home, and no one on the outside would notice. The thick walls of my castle were—"

He cupped one hand over his mouth for a moment, his cheeks turning red.

"Do not feel embarrassed," Henry said. "We are brothers now."

" 'Brothers now'. . ." Selwyn repeated, savoring those two words. "Henry, Henry, you cannot know how that touches my soul."

He tightened his own grip on Henry's hand.

"But I am so apprehensive about reaching out," he said.

"I could make a fool of myself in front of others. No one would respect me."

"If those men are going to know you well enough to respect you," Henry told him, "they will also accept your freedom to play the role of a fool now and then. Whatever you do, their respect is bound to be heightened because you have allowed yourself that kind of nakedness in front of them."

"I remember—" Selwyn started to say.

"Go ahead," Cyril remarked. "Nothing goes beyond us."

"I remember how it was when my parents were alive. It was so good to love them, and be loved in return."

"But, my brother, they are *not* alive. You cannot allow yourself to go to the grave with them. Is that the legacy they would have wanted to leave behind?"

Selwyn had thought about that often. And he knew the answer.

"No, it surely is not," he replied.

"Then the best thing you can do is be alive, as living was meant to be."

"But there are only poor folk around here. How many of the poor do you count as friends, Cyril?" Selwyn asked pointedly but with no harshness, for he intended no insult.

"*My* life is not the issue, Nigel. But I will give you this: I do have a full life, and it is that which you have denied yourself."

He then lowered his voice.

"My wife. . .my daughters. . .my friends fill it amply."

Selwyn nodded. "I meant no disrespect. You are right, of course. I have around me only those who are paid to—"

"Change that, too," Cyril interrupted. "Is there any law or any other reason except social convention that demands that you avoid *all* friendships with those on your staff, in particular the knights, most remarkable the lot of them?"

"I have not thought of that, really. I only know from what little I have seen of other lords. But then, Cyril, are you speaking from experience or theory only?"

"I do have a very good friend among the latter on my

estate. He has been with me for many, many years. We go hunting together. We fish together. Have you ever considered that, Nigel?"

"You mean Erik Lofton, I assume."

"That is precisely the man I have in mind."

"I could talk with him, I suppose."

"And I have spoken with the other knights as well. After yesterday, you have their affection and respect."

At first Cyril had greeted this charade of Nigel Selwyn's with considerable pity. It was, after all, a form of self-deception to live surrounded by pretense as he did, imagining that the glorious days of centuries ago could be recaptured in some fashion. The result seemed not one of grandeur, but instead the pitiable delusion of a man with serious psychological and emotional problems.

And yet, he saw how well treated the men were, and how pleased they seemed to be harking back to a time when they were accorded far greater respect than policemen, their "contemporary" counterparts.

"Their affection?" Selwyn repeated, as though the word were a strange one, and he was not quite sure of its meaning.

"Yes, I said affection, and I meant it," Cyril continued. "Bravery is everything with such men. Most worked as bobbies in and around London, as did my guards. After they retired, for whatever reason, they got jobs doing what they do for you and me and others like us. They faced the worst scum imaginable and did so with courage. As far as *your* men are concerned, you went beyond anything they themselves had ever done, beyond bravery itself."

"You lost me just now."

"Is it bravery for a man who has been *trained* to be brave, bravery instilled in him from his youth? Or is it mere reflex?"

Selwyn had been given enough painkiller before, during, and after the operation to induce a state of substantial grogginess. Even so, he seemed to have an uncommon hold on rationality.

Is it bravery for a man who has been trained to be brave,

bravery instilled in him from his youth? Or is it mere reflex?

Selwyn nodded as the truth of what Cyril was telling him became clearer by the moment.

"I am beginning to understand," he said, his voice strained. "My only regret is that you are here after more than half my life has gone by."

"A brave act, however spontaneous it might seem," Cyril continued, "does require the most serious thought, and takes true courage and a conscious act of will. And it does not spring from infertile soil, if I may put it that way.

"You went through all of that yesterday in front of scores of witnesses, Nigel, paying for your bravery with your blood and the near loss of your life. Surely you cannot believe that this was something performed only by rote, for you have conceded that it was the first time in your life that you had felt driven to any such behavior."

"I may not do it again," Selwyn acknowledged sardonically.

"You never *have* to as far as those so-called knights are concerned. But the knowledge that you are *capable* of doing so should be an encouragement. No one is a hero one day and transforms himself into a coward the next."

Selwyn seemed like a man who had been thirsty for a long time and could hardly wait to put a cup of water to his lips.

"Oh my. . . ."

"Pain?"

"Much pain, in my leg and elsewhere. It will be like this for days."

"Should we stay?" Cyril asked.

"No, you must not," Selwyn pleaded anxiously. "Your loved ones are awaiting you. They are certain to be feeling great pain of their own, not knowing, after all this time, what has happened to you. Go back to them. Do not delay another moment."

They did not move.

"I am serious," he said. "*Go!*"

As both men turned to leave the hospital room, Selwyn added, "And if either of you think of me someday, and have the time, come back and pay me a visit. But if I should never see you again, I will understand."

Cyril and Henry knelt by the bed, and the three of them engaged in prayer before saying good-bye.

"Can it be possible that I am suddenly able to love two complete strangers who have come into my world out of nowhere, and cause me to feel like this after so little time has passed, while looking back on half a century of not reaching out beyond the walls of a fortress?" Selwyn told them as they stood. "I once wondered if I could love at all. Now God has shown me that I can, and it is wonderful, gentlemen, wonderful beyond my paltry ability to describe it."

He cast a glance toward the tiny window in that bare room.

"They await you, those brave, fine souls," he said, pain and tears making his voice quaver. "They are good men, Lofton and the other one. You can trust them. They will serve you during the journey home as they have me."

"Will you be all right?" Henry asked.

"I pray so, dear. . .friend."

Selwyn tried to raise himself up from the bed but could not, so Henry bent down over him.

"If only. . ." Selwyn started to whisper into the other man's ear.

"Do not punish yourself," Henry said softly. "I have a few 'if onlys' of my own. If only my mind were more normal. . .if only my brother whom I loved so dearly were still alive—"

He could not continue.

A few seconds later, he managed to say, "Those 'if onlys' can eat you up, sir. You must no longer give in to them."

At that Henry and Cyril walked out into the corridor.

"He will have to change the way he has lived for so long," Cyril remarked. "Otherwise he might as well never be buried. That castle will become a tomb."

"I wonder what I would be like if I had wealth," Henry mused.

"And I wonder about being poor. But we are where God wants us, it seems."

"Do you remember what Paul wrote to the Philippians?"

"Yes, and I think I know what verses you are recalling. 'I have learned, in whatsoever state I am, therewith to be content.'"

They walked out of the hospital, then stood quietly for a moment, their arms resting on one another's shoulder, prepared, they thought, for whatever happened next.

Waiting outside the hospital were Erik Lofton and another knight named John Mottershead, a man so thin that he seemed incapable of lifting a sword, along with the driver who had been assigned to the sleek sedan.

"Is Lord Selwyn feeling better?" Lofton asked.

"Yes, he is," Cyril replied.

"Praise God."

"You care about him?"

"I do."

"He did not appear to be in any way the sort of man who could be loved, before all this happened, that is."

"Lord Selwyn has never been less than kind to my comrades and me," Lofton admitted. "We are fortunate to be with him."

"But he seems to feel that he is completely alone."

"All of us who serve him as protectors have tried again and again to show Lord Selwyn how we feel, but he has not been willing to listen other than with the politeness that his social position has dictated.

"Mind you, he is never nasty, but just thanks me or one of the other men, smiles predictably, and walks off, and that is the end of it. He has made his pursuit of privacy the only thing that matters, and he has closed the door on anything else."

"I suspect all that may be quite different now," Cyril suggested. "It may be quite different indeed for all of you."

He wished he could tell the man the unspoken part of what he meant, that portended catastrophe which might soon engulf virtually every country in Europe, and force families and governments to show pretense.

"I hope so, Lord Fothergill," Lofton said. "It would be a pity for a man like that to spend the rest of his life the way he has been. A waste!"

In the distance, atop the white hills of Dover, while that castle could not be seen, its presence could be felt as an imagined gloomy specter symbolizing one man's self-imprisonment.

"His prison still?" Cyril asked.

"Not if I have anything to do with it," Lofton said.

"But will he listen?"

"Can Lord Selwyn afford not to listen?"

"I doubt that he can."

"Will you pray for us?"

"I shall."

And Henry added, "I will, too."

"He has no friends, he says," Cyril interjected.

"I have to be very careful," Lofton acknowledged freely. "For one thing, I must never appear to be insolent."

"That is very true," Cyril agreed. "We are bound by our traditions. They are central to our way of life. And woe to the one who tramples them underfoot."

However sincere the friendliness that might exist between individuals from different classes, it was superficial at best. True *intimacy* of any kind had to be discouraged, and along with it, any conduct or speech that could be deemed rude or disrespectful if it emanated from members of the underclass, though any man or woman of nobility could get away with coarse behavior whenever they wished.

So it was that Erik Lofton, for the sake of his own future, had to avoid creating any impression suggesting that he was *demanding* anything, this despite the fact that, as a tacit tribute to their certified valor, knights could take certain liberties, and yet there remained lines of conduct and conversation that could not be crossed.

Until Selwyn himself wished this to happen.

"It is something to look forward to upon my return," Lofton said dryly.

"Which route should we take?" Cyril asked, deciding to change the subject.

Lofton had been thinking about that for some time.

"The one past Woodhenge, I suspect," he replied. "I have usually avoided that spot because of its occultic history, but it might be a useful route for us now. If the forces, human or demonic, allied against you are on the move, the shorter our route, the better. It seems to me that a longer trip offers its own hazards. Besides, I know of no recent activity in the area of Woodhenge."

"That does save some miles."

But the knight could tell that Cyril did not embrace the idea.

"You do not seem overjoyed, if I may say so," Lofton observed. "May I assume that you are recalling the evil history of that location?"

"You may, and I am," Cyril replied forthrightly. "I have always been of the opinion that the Druids were far more evil than history and today's political correctness have led us to believe."

"The longer we find ourselves on the road, *any* road, the greater the danger."

"I bow before your unassailable wisdom in this matter," Cyril acknowledged graciously.

"I do not intend to appear as though I know more than you, sir," Lofton said, flustered, mindful of the protocol that existed between a knight and a lord, even a "pretend" one such as he.

"But you speak correctly. How can I be upset by someone who is using that knowledge to save my life?"

"As you can see, noon has already passed, and we should be on our way," Mottershead interjected rather nervously, the pale skin of his long, narrow face making him seem even less robust than his bony frame did.

Lofton nodded, and the other man effortlessly mounted his horse.

"I can see that you are surprised," Lofton noted.

"The man seems almost sickly," Cyril whispered, offering no pretense.

"Rest easy, Lord Fothergill. John is far more than that, in addition to being an absolutely fearless man. If he were surrounded by a dozen of the enemy, he would not be one to panic but stand his ground.

"I did feel as you when I first met Mottershead. Forget what his outer appearance suggests. The man has sufficient strength for any reasonable demand but something as well, apart from his courage, that none of the rest of us possesses."

"What would that be?"

"Speed and agility. You would be astonished, in plain terms, just how *quick* John Mottershead is. The swiftest of hares have nothing on him. Indeed, the rest of us seem like tortoises compared to the way he is able to move. Astounding!"

Lofton paused, studying Cyril.

"There is something else, is there not?" he asked.

"I have to say that you are correct."

"May I ask, sir, what that is?"

Lofton had been persuasive regarding the other man's abilities and his relentless valor. But concerns lingered about something else.

"How can someone who is as thin as he hope to survive if our country is ravaged by any epidemic? Is he not doomed, poor man? This concern is not for today, during our little journey, but a year from now, two, three years."

Cyril was thinking of Sarah, his frail daughter. He had fewer doubts about Clarice.

John Mottershead was growing impatient.

"May we go. . .at last?" he asked tartly.

Cyril and Henry climbed into the car.

"More discussion later?" Cyril asked as he nodded at Lofton.

"If you would honor me in that manner," the knight said.

"I would."

"Then I look forward to it, Lord Fothergill."

And then the final leg of a long odyssey began.

The two modern-day knights were asked by Nigel Selwyn to use their horses during the journey. Cyril felt that this was an unduly pretentious request but their benefactor insisted, indicating that his men were well-known throughout the region, and that, even in present-day England, would not stir up any attention because he had ridden in the car that was being provided—a late model Jaguar sedan—on those occasions when he did venture outside his estate. The two knights and he were a feature of the countryside, and people would assume that it was Lord Selwyn in the car as always.

Cyril reluctantly agreed that this made sense, that no one would be expecting anybody else apart from Selwyn himself.

The two horses chosen were magnificent steeds, with full medieval saddles and other embellishments, including colorfully adorned pouches on the sides of each animal. Cyril had no idea what was inside, but he decided that he did not need to know.

As children along the route waved to them, it seemed as though the way home would be free of any obstacles.

CHAPTER 7

It would seem that the need to remain as nondescript as possible was not served well by the sight of two knights on horseback riding next to a late model automobile, and yet all the Selwyn pseudo-knights were such familiar figures in that locale that they were certain to not draw any real attention at all. Though Selwyn's conceit was well-known and often viewed with affection, many were aware of his acts of kindness toward the poor as well as toward deserted animals. Years before, Selwyn had created a small zoo of sorts on his property, populated by rare creatures and exotic birds as well as ordinary cats and dogs. He took care of them for many years, eventually giving up as he became too grief-stricken when, one by one, they died. For him, they were a family over which he had charge, and losing any became unbearable.

Chanting. . .the sound seemed to be carried by a breeze, not a sweet sound, like a bird's song or someone playing a tender melody on a flute, but ominous, dispiriting.

As the travelers stopped to stretch their legs, the strange chanting reached their ears, then faded away, until it was heard again seconds later.

A call to darkness. . .

"You know what that is, Lord Fothergill?" Erik Lofton asked, his weary manner suggesting that the answer was an old story to him. "Can you guess, sir, its purpose?"

"I know nothing about the sound, except how it affects me," Cyril replied.

"How *does* it affect you?"

"Like being trapped in a roomful of rats."

"That is what it is supposed to do, sir, by its very sound . . .tap into the worst fears of anyone who is its target. The chant you hear is called *diablerie*."

"What does that mean?" asked Cyril.

"A summoning of evil, a call to the diabolical forces that roam this world, seeking whom they may devour, now and for eternity. Another age-old name is *kosmokratoras*."

Stronger, more insistent, changing somehow, like an opera singer switching from a soprano's voice to that of a baritone.

"Different now," he muttered. "They—"

Lofton gulped, shedding the image of ever-present bravery.

"Forgive me," he said, aware of how he was reacting. "I can run a gauntlet with less fear than I am filled with when I hear that."

The knight's expression made Cyril uneasy, but enabled him to delve into a subject that had long fascinated him. . .the study of an ancient sect named the Druids.

He suggested this to Erik Lofton.

"How did you know, Lord Fothergill?"

"It seems rather obvious, frankly. This used to be where they were most active, I gather, at this and other sites around England. And there was something else that alerted me."

"What was it?" Lofton asked.

"That look on your face."

"I am seldom so obvious, Lord Fothergill."

"Tell me what you know."

"It sounds so much like their most dreadful chant, more severe than the previous one, a chant intended to summon a soul from one body into another."

"But I thought the Druids, in any effective way, had faded entirely, buried as they should have been by the advent of Christianity."

"That was what I was taught. But now how can any of us be sure? The chants they are making are unmistakable."

"Could another group simply be borrowing from their rituals, imitating the Druids perhaps, trying in fact to throw off anyone who stumbles upon them?" Cyril offered.

"That might be the most sensible explanation," acknowledged Lofton, while not being thoroughly convinced.

"May I suggest something else?" Henry then asked a bit uncertainly.

The others nodded.

"My brother was interested in the Druids as well. He became quite certain that their kind had sailed from England and settled on the continent, spreading heresies everywhere. Everyone else thinks they ceased to exist altogether. But not Maximilian Letchworth, oh, no!"

"They left here and took up elsewhere?" Lofton asked, considering that possibility. "That makes sense; that makes a great deal of sense."

"The seeds of evil spreading. . ." Cyril muttered. "Heresies deceive and bring forth evil fruit, men and women so covered by darkness that the promise of heaven is taken from them, and instead they are sent on the road directly to hell. And now that something surpassingly dark and unholy is afoot, they are on the way back, with this location just one of the outposts that they intend."

Henry had a chilling thought.

"I wonder what would happen if they are able to link up with this Gervasio you mentioned?" he asked.

"Evil attracts evil, vultures around a carcass," someone else's voice muttered, taking the rest of them by surprise.

It was John Mottershead, the other knight, who now joined in with the conversation by introducing that remark.

"And what carcass is that?" Cyril asked.

"The civilized world, Lord Fothergill."

The images that came to his mind were vivid, and consistent with what Cyril had learned during the outgoing leg of his odyssey.

"But who actually started it, this idea of widespread vengeance?" Lofton asked of everyone, including himself.

"You would think the Muslims," Cyril speculated.

"And not the Druids, who are nearly as logical as candidates?" Mottershead posed. "Their religion supposedly died out after the Celts became Christians. These early Christians outlawed the worship of many gods, the idea of a soul dying only to pass on to another body, and other important facets of Druid beliefs, including the fanatical pursuit of astrology, pantheism, and sorcery, as well as human sacrifice. But if Henry here is correct. . ."

"It sounds as though you have studied a great deal about the Druids," noted Cyril with some appreciation.

"I have," Mottershead said. "My great-great paternal grandfather was one of the few remaining Druids."

"I thought the sect had been banished well before the twelfth century," Cyril questioned.

"The few who stayed in England went underground, and I mean literally underground. There are passageways connecting most of their sites throughout this country. These invariably lead to large caverns where small groups of Druids were able to gather beyond the sight and hearing of anyone who was not a member."

The chanting was heard again. . . .

"Did they ever sound like that?" Cyril asked.

"Yes, Lord Fothergill, apparently the original Druids did, according to what my grandfather told me. He could imitate the sounds, and what he demonstrated was very much like what we are hearing this very moment."

Cyril listened more intently.

"But the ceremony or whatever they are doing here seems not to be underground now," he pointed out.

"They may feel emboldened," Mottershead speculated.

"But why?"

"Some Europeans are convinced that evil acts are on the increase, that the established church is less effective a bulwark against superstition, crime, perversity."

The chant was not wholly repetitive but seemed instead like an occultic version of a Christian hymn.

"The language itself sounds unfamiliar," Cyril observed, "a mixture of Gallic and whatever else. Can you translate, Mr. Mottershead?"

The other man nodded.

"They are singing about themes perpetual for the Druids.

They believe in magic, in so-called powers held by plants and animals."

Cyril immediately raised another notion.

"Sounds like the New Agers," he pointed-out, "with their Mother Earth theme, and all those other aspects. . .holy crystals and the rest."

"Agreed!" Lofton exclaimed, and with some contempt. "I can only believe that they also must represent a large percentage of that group of deluded souls who choose to worship whales."

Cyril spoke up then.

"Henry and I have recently had the most wondrous experience with these spellbinding animals, but we have not succumbed to putting them on some kind of pedestal, nor do we elect to bow down before any graven images of them. Such deluded fanatics!"

"The original Druids went so far as to profess the greatest possible reverence for mere oak trees and mistletoe," Mottershead added. "Many of their women became sorceresses or what also might be called witches.

"My grandfather used to say that *his* great-great-great-grandfather would tell him that the Druids planned on staying dormant, like slumbering bears hibernating during the winter, until the time for fresh new evil had arrived, and then they would reemerge, driven by the moral and spiritual conditions of the times."

Two fanatical groups, antagonized by the outreach of Christianity, could now be combining their hatred into a single malevolent force.

"Is there anything at all that would prevent the Druids from forming a relationship of necessity with the Muslims?" Cyril asked, barely able to speak the words. "Are there any issues existing between them that would disrupt an alliance?"

"Nothing that I can see, Lord Fothergill," Mottershead replied. "If anything, they are ideal partners, that is, until the war against western civilization has been won and the Muslims decide that the Druids have outlived whatever usefulness they had. After all, cooperation between the Nazis during World War II and what became the political party of Saddam Hussein occurred out of mutual interests. Why not this?"

"They would betray their partners?"

"The Druids would be, to the really devout Muslims, little more than just another group of infidels, infidels unencumbered by anything truly Christian or Jewish, for that matter, but roundly condemned by Allah in the Koran, their holy book.

"It is likely that they would attempt to slaughter every last one of the Druids, though that is certain to spark a frightful war that would make the Crusades seem like nursery tales for impressionable children."

Cyril had not considered that possibility.

"Why do you say that, Mr. Mottershead?" he asked naively. "Is there no end to the bloodthirstiness of either?"

"Human life has never been sacred to either the Druids or the Muslims," the knight went on. "Both cling ferociously to a belief in the deliberate shedding of enemy blood, and the more this happens, the better.

"The Druids regularly kidnapped and murdered—they would say sacrificed—as atonement for those suffering from grave illnesses or physical conditions because their religion seemed to teach that this was how healing was obtained from the gods."

Henry steeled himself for the next revelation.

"Is there more?" he asked, his eyes bloodshot.

"Their favorite means of sacrifice were large wickerwork images, sometimes called wickermen," Mottershead told him and the others. "The Druid priests forced two or three or more victims into each of these, and then set fire to the wicker, while they stood back and enjoyed the screams of the dying."

To gain *pleasure* from the shedding of blood seemed so alien to Cyril that he tried to dismiss that idea as unreasonable, but could not because the other man sounded convincing enough to be given all the credibility required for anyone else to accept everything he said.

"For the Muslims," Mottershead added, "murder is a completely acceptable, even preferred means for achieving what they seek. Anything else leaves open the possibility that the enemy might escape. They use anyone they wish and then dispose of that person, that group, that nation as so much garbage."

"Do you know why they do this?" Lofton asked.

"What they seek is the elimination of all infidels," Mottershead declared. "I am convinced that nothing less can be tolerated as far as they are concerned, even if it means that millions of their own will be sacrificed at the same time."

"Shouldn't we avoid going any further along this route?" Cyril asked.

"It would mean retreating half the distance we have come already, and then going the longer way around that we wanted to avoid. Besides, when they are into their ceremonies, it seems to me, it is almost as though they have been hypnotized, for the outside world ceases to matter. We should be able to slip past without attracting any attention."

A short while later, after they had resumed their journey, the driver stopped the automobile in which Cyril and Henry had been riding, with the two so-called knights on either side with their Selwyn-mandated horses.

"May I take care of myself?" he asked, his need appearing to be an urgent one.

Lofton gave the man leave.

He opened the door, and walked quickly across the dirt road to a sheltered spot among the trees on that side.

"How many more miles?" Henry asked while they waited.

"Til we pass Woodhenge." Mottershead replied.

"Yes. Is it soon?"

"Just ahead," Lofton replied. "Less than a mile."

The chanting now started up again, growing louder and sounding somehow more harsh.

Anxious to continue, they waited for the driver to return. More time passed.

"I think we should go look for him," Lofton advised. "Is that all right with you, Lord Fothergill?"

Another man, in circumstances akin to those, might have lost patience, ordered his guards to forget about the driver, and take him the rest of the way home without further delay, for if the man were insolent enough to treat someone of noble birth so thoughtlessly, he deserved to be inconvenienced himself when he finally decided to come back out of the woods after doing what it was that he had done, and found nobody waiting for him.

Cyril *was* tempted to issue such a command, and for good reason. He had had to endure more than most men in a lifetime and, as a result, was feeling so tired that he was close to collapse, despite the brief respite at Selwyn's castle. But he stopped himself from giving in to the kind of arrogance that was commonplace throughout England.

"Let my friend and me join you," he offered.

Lofton nodded, grateful to have their cooperation.

"I thank you for that, sir. I really had no right to ask anything of the sort, I mean, from someone of your station," he added, meaning no sarcasm.

Cyril dismissed the matter as trivial.

"You were promised candor," he reminded Lofton, "and you have indulged me, my good man, which is fine."

The four of them walked anxiously across the road and discovered a narrow path through the gathering of trees.

Footprints. Not just one set of prints but several.

"Listen!" Lofton said.

Cyril and Henry stood without moving or breathing, waiting to hear what had caught the knight's attention.

Nothing. They could hear nothing.

"What are you talking about?" Cyril asked irritably.

"You hear no birds, do you?"

Cyril listened again, while wondering if Lofton were engaging in some kind of game, the purpose of which was known only to him.

"I do not," he admitted.

"Nor any breeze moving the leaves on the trees?"

Cyril glanced at several of the trees.

"Not a single leaf, as far as I can tell."

"I agree," Mottershead commented. "But here is something else. The animals, Lord Fothergill, the animals."

"What about them?"

"No animals are scurrying through the undergrowth."

Cyril was losing whatever patience he had managed to hold onto.

"My answer is the same. Please, tell me now, what *are* you getting at?"

"Listen again, if you will, Lord Fothergill."

Cyril humored him but the result was the same.

"I hear no signs of—" he started to reply.

"Life, sir?" Mottershead spoke. "Where is it? I hear no indication of any kind that says there is a single living thing where we are."

He walked over to one of the trees and reached for a lower branch, breaking it in half, then holding the piece in front of the other men.

"Dead," he told them, and handed it over to Cyril who examined it, then passed it to Henry, and finally came Erik Lofton's turn to examine the five-inch-long section of tree branch, which he did, turning it over and over.

"John is right," he said. "Look!"

He pressed two fingers against the wood and it turned instantly to crumbled matter, like ancient dust, dropping straight to the ground.

"Look at how it falls," he remarked, "as though there is no air to carry it. It drops like a far heavier substance."

Cyril spotted something else and bent down, stirring the leaves at his feet as he gathered some of the soil in his hand.

"Notice the color," he said, holding the dirt in front of him.

"Gray," Lofton noted.

"Like ashes," Henry suggested, a look of growing fear on his face, twisting his lips unevenly.

They looked around on the ground and saw that wherever it was not covered by leaves, the same gray material was visible.

"Under that pile of leaves to my left," Lofton pointed. "Is that a—?"

The knight brushed the leaves aside.

"I thought so!" he exclaimed.

Lofton stepped back so the others could see what he had noticed. . .a skeleton, a complete human skeleton.

Henry gestured in another direction.

"Over there," he said. "I think I can see another one in the middle of that pile of rocks."

It was Mottershead's turn to find out.

Henry's perceptions proved equally sharp.

But there was a difference this time, something that hinted at the more recent disposal of that particular body.

Long, thin worms were crawling out of the empty eye sockets.

Mottershead stepped back in disgust.

"Notice something that is the same about both of them?" Cyril asked.

"Their bones are tinged with soot but not quite turned to ashes," Lofton said.

Sacrifices. . . .

Mottershead dug his foot into the dry, powderlike ground in anger, revulsion, and not a little fear.

"Barbarians!" he exclaimed. "They are as evil as my family said. . .possessed by demons from hades!"

Some dirt had been dislodged.

"*Look!*" Henry screamed, pointing toward the knight's foot.

The outline of a human skull. . .buried inches below the surface.

Mottershead saw it now.

"I wonder. . ." he speculated, "if this whole area may be a burial ground for the hapless victims of Druid rituals?"

"Over here," Lofton said. "Near me."

A clump of bushes, brown and stiff and brittle, dead like

the rest of the once vibrant growth in this dense miniature forest.

"Inside," he said as the others came over to him.

Bodies. More bodies. Or what was left of them. Tiny, so tiny. The remains of children, the bodies of babies.

"The bones have been burnt," Henry noticed. "I see the blackened edges, the—"

He turned away, unable to bear the sight any longer.

"When a pregnant woman who was judged to be useless to the Druid cause was picked for sacrifice," Mottershead told them, "her baby was cut out of her womb and placed as a separate offering on an altar of wicker."

He looked from Cyril to Henry to Erik Lofton.

"They were so pleased at times like that!" he exclaimed, tears stinging his eyes. "It meant that they had two victims for the effort to secure just one."

He banged his fist against a tree next to him, nearly breaking his fingers, causing a cloud of brown dust to hit the air.

"Ghastly monsters, every last one of them!" he cried out. "But they are so blind, so demonized, that they cannot see this. Druids think that they are adhering to some kind of pantheistic righteousness, that their tree and animal gods are applauding their actions but especially the one that they consider the most powerful, this earth, this world itself. They think of it as Mother Earth, for from it they were born and to it they shall return."

The New Age amuck, revealing its true satanic self!

Lofton tried to calm him down but Mottershead would not listen.

"If you only knew what they are *really* capable of," he went on. "If you only knew the kinds of evil acts that they engaged in hundreds of years ago, and yet, even Julius Caesar, as brilliant as he was, fell under their spell. He went so far as to put them in charge of all Roman sacrifices, public and private.

"Druids were the real cause of the later persecution of Christians, since Romans had been innately tolerant of all sects, and it is likely that the slaughter of so many Followers of the Nazarene, as Christians were first named, would never have happened otherwise.

"You see, Druids were smart enough to recognize the threat to their survival that Christianity represented. It was they who caused Rome to be burned, and persuaded Nero that Christians were to blame. It was they who instigated the slaying of Peter and Paul and the other apostles. It was they who demanded the exiling of John to Patmos.

"And they could do all this, achieve all this, without senators and centurions and others of conscience ever finding out, because all their meetings were conducted in secret, usually in the midst of Roman forests where they passed the verdicts of innocent men, women, and children who were powerless to stop them."

The men decided to go over the terrain for a dozen feet in each direction, recoiling at their discoveries.

Additional remains.

"A child," Lofton said, his face looking oddly bloodless. Hours before, he had appeared robust. "There is the skeleton of a child here."

He dug deeper.

"God in heaven!" He fell back against the ground.

"What is it?" Cyril asked.

"There! Look! The work of Satan himself."

Not just a single child. Several small bodies, as many as half a dozen.

"We *have* to find our man," Cyril said. "He may need our help. How can we just abandon the poor fellow?"

The others murmured agreement and left that one location, aware that under their feet, wherever they stepped, might be other skeletons.

It did not take long. Less than a minute passed before they finally found the spot where the driver had taken care of his needs.

Henry looked up, saw some light ahead, and pointed in that direction.

It seemed only a short distance.

"Fire," Cyril said. "Something is on fire."

Orange-red colors.

Flickering, like dancing flames. . .

"It might spread through the woods," Henry said. "Should we not be getting out of here, and alert the proper authorities?"

"It depends, my brother. Perhaps it is only a campfire."

"Far too large for that," Henry cautioned. "It is something more than that, dear friend, a great deal more."

They could hear the intense crackling sound of something burning, not at all like a simple fire around which people warmed themselves.

Shapes. Shadowy figures. A multitude of shapes moving ahead of them.

"See the moon!" Henry exclaimed like the child that part of him was, as he looked toward the night sky. "The moon is full this night."

He stared at it for a moment, then added, "Even my rational brother thought that evil was transcendent during nights such as this."

Cyril felt himself increasingly becoming a substitute brother.

"Just superstition," he retorted. "By thinking that way, we are only playing into the hands of whatever evil forces might be loose."

The figures ahead could be glimpsed through scattered openings in the thick growth of that section of forest, which reminded Cyril of the legendary Sherwood Forest.

"Some kind of ceremony," Cyril said, squinting. "But we are just not as yet close enough to learn more."

As they were cautiously walking forward, neither noticed at first that the two knights had left them. But then Henry turned around to whisper something to Erik Lofton.

Gone. . .

Both Erik Lofton and John Mottershead had vanished.

"They have run away!" Henry proclaimed. "What awful

bloody cowards!"

"Come now, that hardly sounds like knights of the caliber of Lofton and Mottershead—" Cyril then saw that Henry was not mistaken.

"What in the world could have made those two abandon us?"

"They seemed to be friendly, dedicated," Henry mumbled. "How could they do this to us? And why? Why would they abandon you and me?"

"I can think of nothing except the most awful possibility."

That did not make Henry feel any better.

"What is it, Cyril? Tell me."

"They are conspirators."

Henry recoiled from that.

"With the Muslims and the Druids?" he asked.

Cyril had no desire to condemn either of the knights in that way any more than Henry, but he could conjure up no other reason for their behavior—except the one that his friend had blurted out moments earlier, which continued to be unthinkable, the notion that men of valor would fall prey so suddenly to the most blatant display of cowardice.

"But remember, my friend, how Mottershead did seem to be speaking from some resource of special knowledge about the Druids, giving us the sort of information that could hardly have been gleaned from books alone," Cyril reminded him. "Yes, I admit, the reason Mottershead gave for all this sounds quite logical and all that, but since you and I have no *other* explanation, can we dismiss *this* one so easily?"

"I was curious myself," Henry said. "If we had asked him more questions, he probably would have had all the answers."

"And I have to wonder if all of that comes from some nameless relatives in one's family background?" Cyril remarked.

His instincts were almost always noble and grounded in a history of bravery, whether his family was involved or not, but he was never foolhardy, and he knew that the two of them had to leave, and do so immediately, despite abandoning the driver.

"We had better be going back," he urged. "We could become trapped."

Henry had become uncertain and nervous, his mind straining to take in everything that was happening.

"They may be anticipating this, waiting out of sight when we go back the way we came," he spoke. "What are we to do if that is the case?"

Suddenly Cyril put one finger to his lips.

"*Listen!*" he said.

But he need not have said or done anything, for Henry heard it at the same time. Suddenly that dead place seemed more than ever like a strange and forbidding burial field, containing a countless number of bodies.

Just ahead.

A man's screams.

And the musty odor of burning wicker.

Their driver was dying.

If he had not been with us, Cyril thought, *none of this would be happening. Does he leave a family behind, perhaps much like my own?*

The man had been placed inside a tall wicker figure, twice as wide as he was, a figure that looked like a grotesque scarecrow.

He was calling out for mercy as flames sped up the dry wicker, consuming it quickly.

"I have done nothing," he begged them, his voice hoarse. "Why are you people condemning me to death?"

One of the shrouded figures stepped forward, as close to the flames as he dared.

"Are you a Christian?" he asked in a sonorous voice.

"Yes, I am!" the driver yelled proudly.

Cyril could hear that one figure start laughing, the others joining in with him.

"That is why you die, fool!" he replied, throwing his

head back in a gesture of triumph and satisfaction.

Cyril and Henry could do nothing as they watched, for they were outnumbered six to one by men dressed in long, hooded black robes.

"Oh, Lord, Lord, Lord, Lord!" Henry mumbled.

Gripped by a desire to get up and run but frozen in fascination by what they were seeing, the two men were pressed close to each other as they witnessed a rite that the Druids had maintained was intrinsically holy.

"Holy?" Cyril repeated. "It can only be satanic."

Neither of them could be heard above the chanting that had resumed, and the man's dying screams filling the air.

"I think we are at the mouth of hell," Henry said.

A chill rooted in that night of growing evil took hold of their bodies.

"Look, Cyril," the other man said. "In God's name, look at that!"

Hovering just above the clearing where the ceremony was being performed were figures that seemed to glow like fireflies, with misshapen heads and bodies that looked like weathered leather.

The kosmokratoras. . . .

Demons which had been sent by Satan literally to bedevil any human being to whom they could gain entrance.

"I know what they are," Henry whispered fearfully. "My brother once had to confront them while he was sailing past the southern tip of Africa."

He remembered that frightful time well, onboard the ship captained by Maximilian Letchworth for nearly a decade. The encounter occurred in the midst of yet another violent storm at sea. And the crew had just begun to lose its nerve.

That was when the visitation began. . . .

"They appeared from every direction," Henry continued, keeping his voice low. "First when lightning swept down from the sky, and then dancing around the edges of the ship, as though studying us, looking for the weakest link."

"Were the creatures you saw like *those?*" Cyril asked,

indicating the *things* that they witnessed now, hovering in and around the site.

"Exactly like them."

Cyril had known dread often during the past week but never was it stronger than when it grabbed hold of him then.

"What did your brother do?" he asked.

Henry allowed himself a faint smile as his brother came to mind.

"He got everyone to fall to their knees and pray," he said.

"The Lord's Prayer?"

"Yes, but he also had them claim whatever other promises in any other Bible verses they could recall."

"Did that work?"

Henry hesitated. "At first, those creatures seemed not to pay attention. And then, as I discovered later, we all realized that, however horribly they acted, however repugnant their presence, none seemed able to *touch* a single one of us, not the crew, not the captain, no one. We seemed to have an invisible shield around us.

"And yet it was still terrifying, Cyril, watching those twisted, foul monsters as they danced over the heads of every man and once seemed to sit among our midst, sneering as they tried, I think, to scare us out of our faith."

"Doing what?"

"Taunting us, spouting the most vulgar obscenities and profanities, but it was the blasphemies that were what proved the worst."

"You could actually *hear* them?"

"Not with our ears but in our minds, which meant that we could not clamp our hands over our ears and block out the sounds."

"And yet they retreated? They seemed to manifest such extraordinary power and it was all for naught?"

"They did leave, failing in their mission."

"Was it due to your brother's unwavering faith?"

Henry was oddly hesitant.

"Partly that, yes."

"And something else, Henry, is that it? It was not Maximilian alone?"

"The crew members who were there said, later, that *I* had something to do with it, and my brother testified to this."

"Do you know what that was?"

"I suppose. . ." Henry began awkwardly.

"Tell me, my brother."

"While the others were kneeling, I stood, opened my eyes, and dared the legion of *kosmokratoras* to attack me."

Henry was trembling but with excitement rather than fear.

"What did you say?" asked Cyril.

"I claimed the protection of the shed blood of Jesus Christ, and made the sign of the cross on my chest. I then commanded those foul beings to leave but they did not at first; they took my pleas and threw back at me the most unspeakable filth.

"So, I addressed Satan himself directly, though I could not see him among the other demons—even if I had, how would I have known?—but I could sense that he was there. I commanded the devil to get behind us, to leave that ship and all the area around it, and never to return."

That was when something had hit Henry across the chest, knocking him off his feet and sending him sliding from one end of the deck to the other.

"I banged my head and nearly blacked out. My eyes closed briefly and I saw what I think was Satan, looking at me curiously while, it seemed, puzzling out the kind of man I was, though I could be wrong about that. It might have been one of his most hideous demons."

The other crew members were screaming, and more *kosmokratoras* seemed to be gathering, ready for some kind of final assault.

As Henry continued, Cyril almost forgot the reality of what was happening in front of the two of them for the terrifying recollection of his friend.

"I closed my eyes, and asked the Lord for more strength,

more courage, more of whatever was needed to bring honor and glory to His name. When I opened my eyes, I felt the greatest peace of my life. I smiled at what I thought was Satan. *I smiled at Satan!*

"I think of that now, and I can scarcely believe that I did anything like that. But there I was, standing before my brother, his crew, a continuing parade of *kosmokratoras,* and possibly the archenemy himself, with a smile on my face!

"Sweet, sweet peace was filling my soul, Cyril, my hands pressed together as though I were some priest at mass, and tears, oh those tears, spilling so rapidly from my eyes that I wondered if there would be any moisture left in my entire body by the time they stopped."

In an instant, those malignant entities were gone. . . .

Henry grabbed Cyril's shoulders.

"We are what we are, *Christians* by rebirth," he whispered, knowing that every second they stayed in that spot increased the likelihood of being discovered by the Druid priests and sorceresses conducting the unholy ceremony in that clearing. "That means we can resist the evil we see right now if we have faith enough.

"If we do not *attempt* to help that poor man, Cyril, and should we escape, we will never be free of his image in our minds at night, the darkness thrusting his burning face and his anguished screams upon us until we can stand it no longer."

"But my wife, my daughters," Cyril protested. "You have no one left, my brother, and that is a curse but also a blessing. We would be walking into the grip of certain death. I am sure they have more of their wicker figures.

"If we were to die tonight, no one is left who is able to report to Edling about the plague. That one man's life has to be compared to those of many millions in a dozen known countries and perhaps others yet undiscovered."

Henry had been ready to charge ahead, to give up his own life if necessary. But Cyril's reasoning carried with it some logic.

"I think you may be——" he started to say.

And then he hugged himself to keep from shaking.

"What can I do to help?" Cyril asked.

"Nothing. He has stopped crying. He is dead already."

"I know how you feel but—"

Suddenly the chanting that had persisted throughout the ceremony of sacrifice stopped.

"So quiet now. . ." Cyril mused.

"I hope they have not become aware that we are here."

"Now! We should head back now."

"To where?" Henry asked. "Can we expect the car to be where it was, with the horses still tied to it?"

The Druids who had not been facing the woods abruptly turned in that direction.

Cyril saw some of their faces, first the men who were closest, and then the women standing not more than a foot or two behind them.

The Druid high priest raised one arm and pointed toward the trees.

"Intruders!" he exclaimed. "Bring another wickerman. Sacrifice them!"

Cyril and Henry turned to run but stopped, realizing that they needed to have weapons of some sort, however make-shift.

"Fallen branches," Henry barked. "Rocks, anything we can use to strike back."

Cyril grabbed a branch near his feet, thinking that it might turn to dust in his hand but it was heavy and solid, a fine club.

Henry had found a large stone that would crush the skull of any man.

And then they both started to run.

The sound of many footsteps behind them penetrated the woods as the first Druids entered.

Suddenly Henry stopped running.

"Dear God!" he sputtered.

The ground started to collapse. He was being pulled down, sucked into a hole as though he had stepped in quicksand. Cyril followed him seconds later, not a sudden plummeting but slowly, the ground giving way, it seemed, with some reluctance.

And something else, very close, very loud.

Noises. Other noises than what had been coming from the Druids and their devilish ceremony. Even louder than seconds earlier. The pounding of hooves, old dead trees crumbling and hitting the ground, branches snapping. The air was filled with a brownish dust so thick that Cyril and Henry started to choke.

"Look!" Cyril shouted as he glanced frantically over his shoulder while his head was still above ground.

Into the clearing charged two horses, with the riders wearing full battle uniforms, including metal reinforcements around their bodies, each carrying long, thick, sharp-honed swords, which they swung expertly and with fatal impact, while holding onto the reins with their free hands, dropping hooded figures one after the other until the ground was covered with a mixture of blood that turned it into red-streaked muddy puddles.

And then everything went dark for Cyril and Henry. Both men were being dragged underground, foul odors all around them, suffocating from dustlike dirt, and the hint of human ashes getting into their eyes, their ears, rapidly clogging their nostrils, their mouths, their descent speeding up as the tunnel around them opened up wider, nothing to brake their speed.

All the way to the kingdom of the damned.

Not a single Druid remained alive.

When Erik Lofton and John Mottershead were through with them, all eleven were strewn across the ground. Those who did not die immediately were killed minutes later, as the two knights dismounted, and went from body to body, finishing off any who lingered.

"We have to find where the tunnel begins," Lofton urged, "before it is too late."

"I have a hunch," Mottershead said. "Just beyond the altar there is a pile of rocks. I think the opening is behind it."

"We must try. If we do not or we fail, they will die."

Mottershead was right.

Armed with swords and daggers and each with a weapon comprised of a chain and small metal balls hanging from it, with spikes jutting out from each one, the two men lowered themselves into the hole, not knowing if they would perish below. . . .